IT STARTS AT HOME

ISBN: 978-1-7349465-0-5

Cover design and interior formatting:
Mark Thomas / Coverness.com

For my wife, Arielle.

I dedicate this to you.

You were the first person to call me an artist and acknowledge my vision.

More importantly, you pushed me to finish the novel or our newborn baby would have to…if I took any longer!

Cheers!

1
THE BRICK HOUSE

It was the year 1998 in the Weequahic section of Newark, New Jersey. All the trees donned burnt orange leaves at the start of the fall season. The wind blew hard, opening screen doors and knocking over empty trash cans.

Roland Webb was no longer just intrigued by the illegal activity that flooded his community; he was very much involved. Being fourteen at the time, he found himself hanging around some much older guys who called themselves The Bulldogs. One guy everyone called Blue took a liking to him in particular. Blue saw Roland put a pretty good beating on a kid in his class and grew fond of him ever since.

Blue, known for his good looks and light eyes, was nearly six years older than Roland and the leader of the small group of misfits. Blue wore designer brand clothes that most kids couldn't afford. Roland had only seen his uncles wearing expensive clothes up until then.

Blue and his guys were small-time crooks. Breaking into local stores, robbing high school students and buying things with counterfeit money. Blue and his crew of four owned just two pistols, lacking the funds to provide everyone with a gun of their own.

One day, while sitting in Blue's back yard, Blue had thought of a plan that would forever change him and Roland's life.

"Ro, what do you want to do with your life, lil man?" Blue asked as he twirled a gun.

Ro was caught off guard by the question, being that no one had ever asked him that before.

"Hell if I know," Roland stuttered.

"What do you like?" Blue pressed.

"Money. I just want to get money, Blue."

"Like your uncles did?" Blue asked.

"Yeah, they used to get mad money. I want that. They used to have cars, money, everything, man," Roland replied.

Both men laughed as they both shared the same passion in money.

"Well, you can't always do what we do, and if you thinking about following my lifestyle and your uncles', then you're wrong. These streets have an expiration date," Blue said. "Your uncles used to be getting bread, but that all came to an end."

"Only cuz of that snitch that they stomped out for trying to hustle on our block," Roland explained.

"Yeah, but eventually they would have gotten arrested regardless. The cops came about the ass whooping they put on that dude, but they were coming to raid the house, regardless," Blue went on.

"Fucking pigs ruined everything," Roland mumbled.

That was the deepest conversation the two ever had. The tone of the talk reminded him of the ones he would have with his late grandfather, Poppa. The tone was similar, but Poppa would have gotten physical with Roland, knowing he was up to no good.

"And with that said, let's get this money." Blue chuckled.

Blue had come up with a plan for him and Roland to score on some big money. He, like Roland, always was looking for more income. He also got tired of Roland complaining recently about not coming up with bigger schemes for better return.

The heist would not include the other guys in Blue's crew for a few reasons. Blue trusted Roland despite his youth. He also knew that if Roland were to get caught he would be charged as a minor and not as an adult. And most importantly it would be a bigger cash pot to split between just two people instead of four.

The plan was to go to the Clear View Mall and try and learn the schedule of an armored truck. Blue had noticed a female guard would carry a briefcase and pistol through the mall. She would walk at a fast pace, going in and out of the stores, never speaking to anyone. There was another guard. He was equipped with a twelve-gauge shotgun and would never leave the truck.

Blue and Roland would go to the mall nearly every day of the week. The two would watch the guards' every move, to the point they learned their schedule to a tee and how long it took. Not only did they notice the guards' patterns, they learned their tendencies. The male guard who never got out of the truck would often look very sleepy. He always had two cups of coffee in his cup holder, and when he wasn't dozing off, he was watching the birds.

It was November first when Blue decided today was the day to take action. The plan was for Roland to sit outside the mall where the guards parked the truck. Roland would pretend to be a kid selling candy for a fundraiser, and then would distract the male guard while the female guard was inside. After that, Blue would come on the opposite side of the truck and start the robbery.

"Sir, would you like to make a donation to the South Ward Ringers' football team?" asked Roland.

The guard paused for a second, looking unimpressed by the gesture. At that moment, Roland began to doubt whether or not this plan was a good one.

"What you got there?" the guard replied.

"Snickers, M&M's, Skittles …"

"Let me get the Snickers, kid."

The guard leaned over the driver side window, leaving his shotgun unattended for a split second in his seat.

"We also got these, sir!" yelled Blue as he leaped into the passenger window.

Blue had his Glock 19 in one hand pointed at the guard

and his other hand on the man's shotgun. Blue came so fast he scared both the guard and Roland.

"Kid, think about what you doing! Now you can just leave now, and I'll act like nothing ever happened, I swear!" the guard pleaded.

"Shut up, I do the talking, big man!" Blue yelled.

Blue was an angry stickup kid. Something Roland learned was that there were different types of stickup kids, as everybody did the job differently. There were calm ones, angry ones, and those who panicked. Blue was definitely an angry robber.

"Okay, kid, okay, what you want??"

"You know what! Don't play stupid. Where's the money at??"

The guard was very much afraid of Blue. He was shaking and staring at Roland for help.

"You moving too slow!" Blue yelled.

Blue took the end of his pistol and struck the guard in the head. The guard's head began to pour blood almost immediately.

"Now get yo ass up and open up some of these cases and shit!"

At this point, Roland was watching his surroundings. Despite this being his biggest hit, Roland was calm.

"This is what we got, son," pleaded the guard as he handed over two briefcases.

"My partner's on her way with the rest," he explained.

Despite having two cases of what he figured to be filled with money, Blue wasn't satisfied. Blue kept rambling through the truck for more.

"Ight, fuck it," Blue said.

Just as Blue finally ended his search for more valuables, the door to the mall cracked open. It was the female guard, to everybody in the truck's surprise. She must have forgot something because she had never returned to the truck that fast.

The look on the female guard's face was of utter shock. She immediately dropped her briefcase and reached for her firearm. At that very moment, Blue looked at Roland, as he was the closest to the guard and without a doubt the first target she would go for. Their eyes locked for a second. A second that felt like an eternity between the two.

"Shit!" Blue shouted.

Redirecting his Glock from the back of the head of the male guard, Blue quickly aimed toward her and pulled the trigger. The bullet struck her in the neck, splitting her collarbone in half. That moment gave the male security guard a brief chance to take the upper hand on Blue. The man elbowed Blue, causing him to lose control of his weapon. The guard had now retrieved his shotgun while Blue was scrambling for his pistol that had slid under the truck after the blow.

"Hey, now you drop yours before I blow his head off, little one!" the guard demanded.

At this point Roland had his gun aiming directly at the male guard. Roland was no longer calm. His eyes were wide open, but his hand was steady. Roland was a great shot not just for his age but for any age.

"I got the shot," Roland said.

"No, no, just go," Blue said with a tremble in his voice.

"I can do it, I swear!" Roland yelled.

"I will drop him, kid!" the guard shouted frantically.

Blue in his heart knew that Roland probably could have shot the man before the guard could pull the trigger, but for some reason, he was throwing in the towel.

"Sir, let him go, and help her while you still can!" Blue said.

The guard looked at the situation and knew that Blue had a valid point. The female guard was gasping for air in a pool of blood.

"GO!" Blue roared.

And at that moment, Roland's eyes began to fill with tears, as he knew that there was no getting out of this one. There was no way his idol was escaping, and this was the end of the duo. Roland lowered his gun, turned, and took off running as fast as he could, only to look back to see the guard pistol whipping Blue in the head with the end of the twelve gauge.

He made it home to his aunt Michelle's house, but home didn't feel the same. He stared across the street at the front of Blue's house. Why hadn't they talked about a better way to avoid getting caught? Now all that money had escaped 'em. He sat on his front porch, dazed. Roland had finally hit rock bottom. He started to get anxious. Thoughts of his mother, grandfather, and Blue all came to mind. He couldn't stop replaying the days he lost his two caretakers and Blue's arrest. Roland blamed himself. He wished he had done more to change the outcomes.

Roland couldn't escape the facts of the attempted robbery. He couldn't find solace in the past, and he had no idea how he was going to go about living toward some future with nothing to look forward to. Lost again in his memories, he'd gotten his first taste of what his uncles had stoked in him and he liked it, nevertheless.

A little over two years prior to their failed attempt at robbing the armored truck, Roland had found it hard sleeping in a single-family Newark, New Jersey home with twenty-two people. He suddenly recalled the early summer of 1996 because his mother was still alive. Poppa hadn't needed to take on the role of both mom and dad yet. Between grandparents, aunts, uncles, brothers, sisters and cousins, the single-family home had been packed. Each room had two to three people living in it. Each room had housed a fan, as there were no air conditioners to keep cool during the heat wave they had been experiencing.

If he thought about it too much and did the math, right now, he'd realize there were only a handful of them left, and the crowded house had provided a lot better of a feeling than the isolation he felt at the moment after leaving Blue to face up to the heist. He felt a devastating loss.

He remembered how this big house had been known for its cookouts and corruption. From dog fighting, drug dealing to gambling, money had flowed in and out of the Webb's residents.

Roland and Sean Webb had stayed on the third floor next

to the attic. Roland had his own bed just a few feet away from where his brother, Sean, lay. Sean, being eight years old, had shared a bed with their mother. A large hole in the bottom of their room door had been an open invite to the family thieves. The boys' mother had put a padlock on the door, but even that couldn't stop a cousin or aunt from crawling through the gaping hole and stealing CDs and ice tea mix.

Poppa, who had spent sixty of his eighty-one years in Newark as the head of this household, had been a powerful man. He had taken care of his community, helping keep the neighborhood clean and lending a hand to his neighbors. He always gave big donations to the school board and homeless shelters. He was known as a very fair, but firm man.

Poppa would embarrass any of his relatives caught misbehaving. The punishment had taken the form of beatings in front of the house to making someone hold a sign outside with the words 'I like to steal from my family' written on it. Poppa was nothing to play with, despite being very loving.

Roland had never acted out around his grandfather. He had viewed the elderly man like a superhero. Stories of Poppa hitting people always tickled Roland, but more importantly, it reminded him of boundaries. It had reminded him that every action is followed by consequences, consequences that Roland had no interest in.

Poppa had two very different relationships with Roland and Sean. Sean was four years younger, so Poppa had spoiled him more. He would tell Sean that once he got a little bit older he would be harder on him. He would say that as he handed him a dollar.

His interactions with Roland were slightly different. They would talk about sports, but he had made Roland take out the garbage for a dollar. He had made it his job to try to teach him work ethics and discipline.

Poppa had made it a priority to raise his boys into men. He had known that growing up in this part of town was tough. The drug epidemic had damaged nearly every home in the community. Almost every residence in the neighborhood had housed a drug addict and a drug dealer. The Webb family was no different. The issue for Roland and Sean was that the drug addict in their home was their mother.

The boy's grandfather had done his best to teach them independence. It had hurt his heart to see the boys long for a healthier relationship with their mother. They were truly chasing something they could never catch. She was simply a good person with a bad habit. Eventually, the habit would catch up to her.

But Poppa had helped the Webb brothers deal with their first heartbreak when their beloved mother died in the summer of 1996. Addicted to heroin for years, she had finally lost her life because of it. She had spent her final weeks in and out of the hospital, but still nothing could prepare the boys for her death.

After the funeral, everyone had gone back to the house to eat. A big feast of turkey, barbeque chicken, macaroni salad, yams and all kinds of cakes and pies had been served. No pork had been prepared, as Poppa was Muslim. They had played the boys' mother's favorite music while they ate her favorite foods.

Roland had been the only one who didn't partake in eating and reminiscing about her. Instead, he had played with his toy gun, sitting off all alone. Poppa had noticed the twelve-year-old isolating himself.

"Hey, your belly gone go hungry," Poppa had said.

Roland's big eyes had just wandered around the room. He had never known anyone to die besides really old people.

"You hear me?" Poppa had asked as he cleaned his hands.

"I'm not hungry, Pop," Roland had said.

"Boy, you haven't ate in twenty-four hours," Poppa had said as he frowned his face.

The two had just looked at each other.

Poppa had stood up slowly. The bald, brittle man had pointed his finger for Roland to meet him outside.

Roland remembered the two of them sitting on the porch together—their usual spot to talk.

"Talk to me," Poppa had said.

"Why is everyone happy when my mom is dead?" Roland had asked as he began to weep.

"No, son. We are celebrating my daughter's life. We will miss her, of course, but we need to remember the good times we had with her. That's what she would want," Poppa had explained.

"She's in a much better place than here, I tell you," Poppa had said as he lit a cigarette.

"Did she die because she was on drugs? That's what Tony from school said," Roland had mumbled.

Poppa had looked at him in anger.

"Listen to me. Tomorrow … you go to school. And as soon as Tony walks his ass in class you punch him in his nose as hard as you can. And tell your teacher you did that because your grandfather said that Tony needs to mind his damn business. You hear me?" Poppa had declared, putting the cigarette back in his mouth.

Roland had smiled. Both of them had chuckled, despite Poppa meaning every word he said.

"Your mother died because … she did what the hell she wanted to do and was hardheaded," the old man had said as he coughed.

"Are you going to die too, Poppa?" Roland had asked as he twirled his toy pistol.

"Yeah I am. Eventually. We all are. Me, you, Sean. Everyone," Poppa had said.

Roland had raised his head. Again, the seventh grader had cried.

Poppa had realized what he had done.

"See Rowie, the catch about this thing called life, it's not about how long you live, but how you live," he had urged.

"Protect your family, your little brother and yourself. Protect yourself because if you don't, nobody will. You have to exercise, get sleep, drink water, be careful of certain people, places and things. Remember how I told you, you can't eat donuts every day? I was protecting you," Poppa had chuckled as he threw his remaining pack of cigarettes in the trash.

"But even if I do that, I'll still die," Roland had responded.

Poppa had smirked, shaking his head and wiping away his own tears, tears he had held in for years.

"You're smart, son. Yeah one day. When you're really really really old. Even older than me," Poppa had said as he put his hand on Roland's head.

Roland had leaned in and laid his head over Poppa's heart.

Poppa's other daughter, Michelle, had opened the screen door.

"Hey, Dad, why are you having this serious conversation with this little boy?" Michelle had asked.

"Girl, go inside. The hell you know," Poppa had yelled.

She had gone inside, huffy and bent out of shape.

"Son, I talk to you like this because you have to grow up faster than everyone else your age. You just have to grow up a little bit faster," Poppa had said as he picked Roland up.

He had carried the boy upstairs to his room. By the time Poppa had reached Roland's room, the boy was half sleep. He had laid Roland across the twin-size bed.

"Pop, can you stay?" Roland had mumbled.

Poppa had closed the door and lied down next to his grandson. Both of them had slept in the bed that night with heavy hearts. Poppa had not slept in another bed in fifty years, but that night had been an exception. Roland had needed him.

He still needed him now more than ever. He missed the house they had lived in.

2

FIRST TASTE

Four months after Roland and Sean had lost their mother, there had been a knock on the door. Roland's uncle Kevin had walked in and broken the news that would forever change the Webb family.

"Hey ... Poppa passed away," he had said quietly.

Poppa had finally ended his battle with cancer. Some say he died from the disease, others who knew him well, said he died from a broken heart after losing his daughter.

Poppa had been the patriarch of the family until the autumn of 1996. He had paid the bills and maintained order in the house. Only so much would go on while Poppa was around.

Despite being devastated by the news, Roland hadn't cried immediately but had turned over and prayed instead. He prayed for his family. The last thing Roland had remembered his grandfather saying to him was, "You never get over death, you just learn how to deal with it."

The loss of his best friend sent him spiraling. Still, Roland had tried to continue to do the things that him and Poppa had once shared. He had tried watching boxing and horse racing alone. He had even taken out the chessboard and played alone for days. Then, he had given up. It just wasn't quite the same.

"Ro, baby, you okay?" Aunt Michelle had asked one spring day, seeing that he hadn't done a thing all day. Now that they were living with her, it seemed like there were too many reasons to stick to himself.

"Yes," Roland had replied.

The once talkative and witty young boy had not said much since Poppa's passing. It had seemed after the death of his mother and Poppa that he only spoke to Sean. Losing two caretakers suddenly had forced Roland to grow up faster than most twelve-year-olds. He now had to wake up thirty minutes earlier to help get Sean ready in the morning. He still had his chores of taking out the trash and shoveling the winter snow. They were living only two blocks away from the house where he'd been raised.

He was always cranky. A mix between his current situation and new responsibilities had caused the boy to be upset on a daily basis. He would go to school upset. He rarely participated in class and was really short with everyone now.

Often, he had spent his days in class just daydreaming.

It had been the third week of eighth grade, and Roland was

already having a rough day. He had gotten no sleep the previous night, as his cousins and uncles played loud music until four in the morning. Something they had never done when Poppa was alive.

Roland had been sitting at his desk, two chairs away from Tony, the classmate who he had told Poppa about earlier when Poppa was still alive. Roland's eyes had felt very heavy. His head had rocked up and down as he fought to stay awake.

"Look, look at Webb," Tony had said to another student.

Roland had opened his eyes. He had looked away from Tony, trying to ignore him.

"This nigga in here nodding off. He on that stuff, man!" Tony had stated.

The two troublemakers had laughed hysterically.

Roland had turned and looked at Tony—his eyes full of fire, his body engulfed in rage. Roland had never felt an anger like this before. His hands had trembled, and his body had begun to get warm.

Roland had smirked at the boy.

"I got you," Roland had said as he fought back tears.

The bell had rung, and class was dismissed.

Roland had zipped up his winter coat and had walked to the other side of the building where Sean and the third graders had come out.

The two boys had headed home, passing vacant house after vacant house, and one drug dealer and addict after another. Roland had to keep his arm around Sean during the walk home, as per Poppa. Poppa had scolded him about walking ahead of Sean, and Roland always kept it in mind.

The boys' after-school routine had been to stop at the corner store to buy snacks. The boys each got .50 cents from their Aunt Michelle. It wasn't quite the one-dollar bill that Poppa used to give them, but it was better than nothing they figured.

Sean had grabbed the same two BBQ-flavored potato chips he always bought. Roland had been torn, he couldn't decide if he wanted candy or a soda.

"Which one should I get?" Roland had asked his younger brother.

"I don't know," Sean had replied.

"Come on, help me pick," Roland had urged.

"If Pop was alive, you could get both," Sean had mumbled.

Roland had just looked at Sean.

"I know," Roland had said as he rubbed Sean's head.

Roland had put away the candy and walked up to the register. The boys had paid for their stuff and headed out of the bodega. Sean had eaten his bag of chips, while Roland had drunk his soda. The boys were three blocks from the store when Roland made a discovery. Roland had felt something in his pocket. He had reached his dry hands into his jean's pocket and to his own surprise he had pulled out the bag of candy.

"Oooh, how you get Candy and Soda!?" Sean had yelled.

"Oh, I thought I put it back!" Roland had said in shock. The boy had accidently taken the candy out of the store.

Roland had paused. Thoughts of what he should do had

filled his mind. Should he take it back? Or just keep it? What would Poppa say if he knew he stole, whether it was a mistake or not? For some reason, Roland had made a decision out of anger. He had known what he did was wrong, but he wasn't willing to correct it.

"Man, all that candy they got. I did it by mistake," Roland had said as he kept walking home. A small part of Roland had been upset with the fact that he no longer had the dollar from Poppa to pay for both the soda and candy. "He should have paid attention," Roland had continued on about the clerk.

Sean had just looked at Roland in shock. He had never seen Roland steal. They weren't raised to be thieves.

The boys had walked home in silence. Despite Roland keeping the candy, he had not eaten it. Once he'd made it home, he sat it on his desk, still torn by his decision to not return the treat.

Three days had gone by. It was a Friday night, and Aunt Michelle had left the boys to fend for themselves as she attended an 80's theme party. Sean had fallen asleep early. Roland on the other hand, had been wide awake, as his stomach was rumbling.

It was nearly midnight, and the last time Roland had eaten was 6 p.m.. He had developed a throbbing headache. Just when he had thought all was lost, he had remembered the candy he had accidentally stolen. Roland had sat up and grabbed the "Fruities" off the dresser. He had finally eaten them. He had felt happy about keeping the candy. If it hadn't been for his decision, he would have still been hungry and waiting for someone to feed him.

Aunt Michelle had had a great time at the 80's theme party, but when she walked in, she looked preoccupied. He had seen her pick up her phone and say, "I know, Sarah, it's just that we aren't getting enough revenue from property taxes right now and so lots of the services that the city normally funded are suffering. It's not like people don't want to support the programs, it's just … well, they're looking to private businesses to help partner up you know, reach out to the community. I feel you. Just let me know what I can do, ok?"

She had hung up the phone and her shoulders had sagged. Then she had gone to bed. Meanwhile, all Roland could think about was how come Poppa gave 'em more to spend.

A week had gone by, and Roland had really checked out at school. Teachers had given up on trying to talk to him during class, even suggesting that he be sent to special education classes. This notion had further frustrated the young boy.

Sean on the other hand, still had been doing well in school. Being that he was younger, he had received the death of two caretakers differently. He had still enjoyed school, as this was a way to get away from his broken home. The idea of becoming anything he wanted in life had still excited him, while Roland was a little bit skeptical about everything now.

It had been a chilly Monday morning. The wind had whistled through the old windows of the Webb's home. The boys had eaten their cereal and quickly watched cartoons as usual. It had been a normal day; Roland had walked Sean to class. Roland had sat quietly throughout the day, and Tony had made jokes about him. Just your typical day.

The only thing different about that particular Monday would be the ending. After school the boys had walked to a thrift store. The boys had come here once with Poppa, so the shop owner knew them.

Sean had been excited to go inside the store. He had loved exploring the old store littered with different equipment and unique items.

Roland, on the other hand, was there on a mission. The twelve-year-old had remembered seeing a pair of brass knuckles for sale at the shop. The only issue, of course, was the fact that he did not have the money to buy it. His plan was to use Sean to unknowingly distract the owner while he pocketed the weapon.

"Hi, Mr. Marshall," Sean had said with a big smile on his face.

"Hey, boys," the store clerk had said as he dusted off the shelves.

Roland had just smiled, not saying a word. He was noticeably nervous. He had never tried to steal something before. He had feared the man, who was Poppa's friend, catching him. However, his fear was minute compared to the anger he had for Tony.

Roland and Sean had both walked around the store—Roland behind Sean. The plan was to tell Sean to ask Mr. Marshall for something, and that would distract him. Just when Roland had gone to give Sean orders, something had come over him. A feeling of guilt. He had thought of Poppa's words of how he needed to protect his brother. He couldn't use him for this.

The boys had continued to examine the entire store. Mr. Marshall and Roland—for a second—locked eyes. Like a teacher making eye contact with a student trying to cheat during a test, he could see that the boy was up to something.

Roland had begun to sweat and tremble. He couldn't stop looking over at the clerk. He was starting to think he should just go home.

Just when his attempt looked like a fail, something unforeseen had happened. Mr. Marshall had gone to the back room, leaving the boys unattended.

Roland was in shock. His eyes were nearly bigger than his face. This was his chance. His nerves were nearly paralyzing. He had wondered, maybe he shouldn't be doing this. He wasn't a thief. And then he had heard Poppa's voice. His voice in his head was nearly as clear as if it was present, saying the words, "...As soon as Tony walks his ass in class, you punch him in his nose as hard as you can." That was enough for the boy. Roland had reached behind the counter and grabbed the all-gold, brass knuckles.

"Hey, Sean, come on, we have to go," Roland had urged.

"Why?" Sean had replied as he spun a globe.

"Come on! Aunt Michelle will kill us," Roland had yelled.

Roland had quickly headed for the door.

"Bye, Mr. Marshall!" the boys had yelled.

The clerk had walked from out the back. He had just stared at the boys heading down the street.

All night, Roland had tossed and turned. He knew he shouldn't have stolen, but he was frustrated with his classmate, and it was time to defend himself.

Roland had bags under his eyes. He didn't get much sleep, and he had a dream about his mom's funeral, which made him weep. At least once a week the young boy had a dream about his grandfather or mother.

The walk to school had been quieter than usual. Sean was his normal self, but Roland chewed on his fingernails the entire walk.

The next day, class had gone as normal. Twenty minutes into the class, Roland picked up his old busted backpack off the ground. He had taken out the stolen brass knuckles from his bag and quickly put them in his pocket. The boy had looked all around the room. His eyes were nearly bulging out of his head. Sweat had literally dripped from his forehead to the pages on his book.

He couldn't do it. He had slowly put the weapon back inside his backpack. This whole situation just wasn't him. Stealing and then attacking someone? That just wasn't who the boy was.

Roland had gathered his things and abruptly left the room.

"Roland, where are you going?" the teacher had asked.

Roland had just looked at her and kept walking.

He had walked to the second floor bathroom to be alone.

The second floor bathroom was filthy. It had smelled of urine and was hardly used by the students for that reason.

Roland had stayed in the bathroom for two hours.

No one had entered the restroom, until two youngsters walked in. It was Tony and another student. They were coming in the bathroom to skip class.

"Oh shit, this nigga Roland in here," the other kid had said.

"Yo, you good?" Tony had chuckled as he touched Roland's shoulder.

Roland had knocked his hand down. He had picked his book bag up and began to leave.

"That dude is retarded, I swear!" Tony had said.

Roland had heard the comment. He had paused at the door. Rather than leave, Roland had locked the door.

The two troublemakers had looked on puzzled. They had never known Roland to be violent, so they lacked fear.

"Say something else!" Roland had said as he began to breath hard.

"What the fuck is wrong with him?" Tony had said laughing.

Roland had quickly reached into his book bag, sliding his hand through the brass knuckles.

"What did you say about my mother?!" Roland had demanded as a tear ran down his face.

Both boys had looked confused, as they couldn't believe he was reacting like this to a comment made months ago.

"I didn't say anything," the second boy had declared.

Tension had been running high. Tony had felt himself

being challenged and now had to stand his ground.

"So, what? You want to fight?" Tony had asked as he took a step closer to the enraged boy.

Roland had finally snapped.

He had head-butted Tony, causing him to stumble backwards. He had dropped his bag. His right hand that had been covered with brass knuckles had struck like thunder, dropping Tony. Having mounted the boy, Roland had banged his head against the dirty bathroom floor.

The other eighth grader just watched in shock. No one seen Roland react to anything, let alone like this.

"Stop!" the boy had yelled.

Roland had finally come out of his trance. He had blood on his hand and shirt. Tony was in a daze.

Roland had stood up.

"Don't ever talk shit about my family again," Roland had asserted.

Roland had put away the brass knuckles and washed his hands. Tony's friend had helped Tony off the ground.

"And y'all better not tell," Roland had said as he stared at the boys.

He had unlocked the door, left the bathroom and then out of the school. He had headed home to change clothes and return to pick up Sean after school. No matter what happened to himself, he could never leave Sean behind.

Roland had taken his brother a different route home just in case Tony came seeking revenge. He had held Sean's hand during the walk. With the same hand he used to assault Tony, he had guided Sean home.

Every time he had wondered whether or not he did the right thing, he had thought of Poppa's talk with him on the porch. He had felt like he had made Poppa proud.

It had been six months since Poppa's passing, and the Webb family had completely spun out of control. Poppa's wife had sold the house and moved out and left the home to the rest of the members. The amount of illegal activity had increased significantly.

Both Roland and Sean were very mature for their ages. Sean would always ask questions about different professional careers from firefighters and doctors to policemen. A few of his family members had always felt the need to tell him to pursue such careers. His aunt, especially, had seen a potential in him that she didn't see in many others. She had received so many complaints from the school about Roland that her belief started to sway in whether or not she could get through to him.

One time he had lashed out at his aunt, telling her, "The only time you speak to me is when the school calls the house."

Roland was ahead of his time. He had a personality that made older folks say, "He's been here before" or "he got an old soul." He would always sit at the table while older family members played cards and gambled. His aunt had known that he used to get in trouble with Poppa because his clothes smelled of smoke from sitting around his uncles as they smoked cigarettes and marijuana, but with Poppa gone, there was no one to discipline him. She had tried occasionally, but it was no use. Roland had sat real close to the crime in and outside of the house, and without Poppa around, it had seemed like he was never going to make better choices.

Both brothers had seen fights, drug dealing, dog fighting, domestic violence and many more crimes. Over the months, gradually, it had seemed like nothing was going to help Roland adjust to life after he'd lost Poppa to his aunt. She had tried. But two years had passed. By 1998, the Webb family had split entirely. Most of the Webbs had scattered all over the state even though the boys still lived in the same neighborhood with her. With the boys' mother gone, their father had moved somewhere down south in the middle of the night.

Their father's absence had cemented itself more firmly in Roland's heart. Being a few years older, Roland had known his father a little bit, while Sean had no real recollection of the man. Rumor had it that he couldn't take the pressure of the death of his children's mother and wasn't looking forward to handling the responsibility of being a single parent.

While Sean wasn't getting into trouble, he was always outdoors. Sean had spent most of all his summers the same way, wandering on Main Street—going inside all the small businesses and talking to the shop owners. He would ask the barbers about cutting hair and the laundrymen about store operations.

Unlike Sean, Roland had gotten himself involved in another kind of business with Blue. The boys' aunt was having trouble keeping up with them. And Roland had spent most of his time totally unwilling to let Sean rub off on him at all but very willing to carve in himself a huge space for how Blue had gone about getting himself properly rich off the streets, and it wouldn't let go of him. No way out, not even after his first taste had been tinged with regret—not about what Blue had gotten them to do but for getting caught.

3

DEATH ROW & LOVE

Ten years had passed since Blue's arrest. By 2008, Roland had really made a name for himself in the city. He had filled out into a grown man. A man with welts on his heart from the ups and downs of life.

Roland was always well-dressed, clean cut. Like his idols, he always wore expensive clothes and jewelry. He was responsible for over half of the robberies in Newark. Now known as "Ro" by most, Roland saw value in everything. He would take drugs, guns, money, phones, bullets, and laptops. Anything you named, Roland would rob people for it.

Crime was at its highest in Newark during the summer time. People were outside all day and the brutal heat made tempers flare. Stickup kids in the past would do nearly all their work at night, but for Roland, the time of day was irrelevant. If it was daylight, him and his crew would just wait until the right time came to get you.

Sometimes Roland would cover his dark-skinned face during the robberies. Sometimes he wouldn't. Rarely did he need to actually use his weapon. Just the mere flash of his Desert Eagle usually got what he wanted.

The last time he had to use his pistol was to push off another stickup kid off his turf. Roland got word that another guy was robbing gas stations in his hood, so he solved it the only way he knew how. He gave the man one offer to get lost. With that attempt having failed, Roland located the competitor and shot him eight times. The threat was eliminated for good.

Roland ran with a small crew that consisted of two others. Ivan Martin was Roland's classmate. He was of African American and Puerto Rican descent and stood about 6' 3". Ivan was a star at the collegiate level and going into his senior year. Talks of him being drafted to the National Football League (NFL) had sped up. Ivan was from Newark but stayed on campus at Rutgers in New Brunswick. He would go back and forth from college campus to the hood throughout the week.

The other kid who was part of the crew was "Lefty." He was four years younger than the other two. His frail frame, tattoo of a cross on his face, a bulldog tattoo on his neck and signature short dreadlocks made him stand out. He was very much into drinking codeine syrup, popping pills, drinking alcohol and smoking marijuana. They called him Lefty because he did everything with his left hand. Everything including shooting his gun. Roland loved Lefty because he saw a lot of himself in him. The same way he had followed Blue around, Lefty began to do that with him. The only difference was that Lefty wasn't truly a gangster. He was a follower being molded into a gangster.

Roland still carried the gang name, The Bulldogs, despite Blue and all of the original crew being either dead or in jail. Roland and his two friends shared similar tattoos to show their camaraderie. Their bodies decorated in gang-related and war-related images and slogans. Roland and his crew had over ten guns combined.

The three of them sat outside the local barbershop on crates as they normally did in the summer heat, discussing their next moves.

"What time is the game?" Roland asked Ivan.

"For the third time, Ro, it's at 1:00." Ivan laughed as he passed the last bit of weed to Lefty.

"You must be catching contact or something," Lefty joked.

The two would always make fun of how Roland didn't smoke. Roland wasn't a smoker because he simply was worried it would turn his lips black or be a gateway drug into doing harder stuff.

"Man, fuck both of y'all." Roland laughed.

Roland wasn't paying them much attention, as he was thinking about his next move.

"Yo, it's been dry around here, man. When was the last time we really hit a lick?" Roland asked the two.

"Hell, we just ran through them boys at the parade. And the

night before was the papi store," Lefty explained.

"Man, that's small money. What did we even get? I don't even remember," Roland replied.

"It's the economy, man. Don't nobody got any money," Ivan said.

Roland just looked at his friend.

"Man, you believe that? The government just be making up shit," Lefty commented.

"It's true," Ivan replied.

"Who told you that? Your mommy?" Lefty poked.

Lefty and Roland often made jokes about Ivan being coddled by having both parents present in his life.

"His real name's Clarence, and Clarence lives at home with both parents," Lefty continued to joke.

All three men laughed at the movie reference.

Roland, listening to his two closest friends debate the impact of the economy, walked over to the sidewalk where a newspaper lay.

At the top of *The Star Ledger,* he read, '*Newark is among worst cities in nation in recovering from economic crisis, study says.*'

Roland just showed his crew the paper.

"People still have money. We just have to find a way to get it out of them," Roland said as he took Lefty's lighter from him. "When people get desperate, ugly things happen," Roland said as he lit the newspaper on fire.

"Dope boys have been profiting off people stressing and getting high," Lefty offered.

Ivan said, "Yeah, but you know I heard something about those new high tech cameras installed in some neighborhoods that cleared out some of them dope boys away from the main streets into the side streets. They've had to move or take business off the streets."

"I ain't seen any of those cameras, but Lefty probably has," Roland said, sneering and acting proud like he'd know how to avoid doing business over drugs better than Lefty did.

Lefty just looked away.

The three continued their conversation about their earnings from the petty robbery.

"Well, I got this," Lefty stated.

Pulling out a silver chain and putting it around his neck, Lefty grinned ear to ear reminiscing about the robbery.

"Man, that cheap shit!" Roland laughed.

"Bro, we risked our lives for three hundred dollars and a funky ass chain?" Roland asked as he shook his head.

There was a pause of silence between the three. The brief moment was shortly interrupted by a roar of engines being revved. It was a roar of over ten dirt bikes coming down the street. It was boys from the West Ward of Newark.

At the front of the line was a kid who Roland had seen before. "What's his name?" Roland asked.

"You know him, Ro. That's James. He played quarterback for my team in high school."

"Oh yeah! That is him," Roland recalled. "Call him over here."

Ivan paused. He was skeptical as to why Roland would want him to come over. Ivan didn't think he would try and rob his former teammate, but he wondered what else could Roland want.

"Hurry up, Ivan! Damn!" Roland said.

"James! What's up, bro? Come here," Ivan yelled.

James looked, paused and turned the corner with all the riders following behind him. Just when it appeared that the bikers were going to keep riding on, they doubled back around to see what Ivan wanted.

James pulled up to the three, leaving his crew several yards behind. His bike was by far the best. It was jet black, no more than ninety pounds, no exhaust and nearly silent. The bike was electric, expensive and one of a kind. Roland couldn't help but show interest in the bike.

"How much you want for that?" Roland asked immediately.

James hesitated for a second. He was fully aware of who Roland was, despite living on the other side of town. James knew that his bike grabbing the attention of a known stickup kid wasn't good.

"This one's not for sale, but I got others I could let you look at," James suggested.

Both Lefty and Ivan looked at Roland, waiting for his reaction to being told "no."

"Cool ... can I ride it at least?" Roland asked.

One could see the sorrow in James' face. He knew that he had made a grand mistake riding his bike through Main Street.

Roland had now stood up and started walking toward James and the bike in sure confidence that he was going for a ride.

"No … not this one, Ro," James stuttered.

At this point Ivan and Lefty both had stood up, preparing for something to happen. All of the other bikers had all stopped riding in circles and had their eyes glued on the two men.

"Oh no?" Roland asked.

Roland began to walk toward the parked car where he kept one of his pistols. The gun was on top of one of the tires, going unnoticed. Just as Roland began to reach for the firearm, he looked up to see a familiar face. It was Mr. Marshall.

It had been twelve years since Roland stole out of Mr. Marshall's store. Five years following that, the older man's shop was boarded up. Mr. Marshall was no longer known for the thrift store he once owned, he was now viewed as just the old man who walked real slow with his cane. In fact his cane was one of the last things he still owned from the store. He wore his usual long sleeve red flannel and khaki pants.

He would walk up and down Main Street, and everyone spoke to him. Having been friends with Poppa and having known Roland since he was an innocent kid, Mr. Marshall was the only one outside of the Webb family who could talk to Roland about life.

Roland and Mr. Marshall had a unique relationship. Outside their relationship with Poppa, they had nothing in common, except the fact that they would talk sports and occasionally play chess together.

"You know what? Cool, James, next time," Roland said as he looked across the street at Mr. Marshall.

James thought Roland was just respecting his wishes to let him keep the bike, but in reality, the only reason he left with that bike was Mr. Marshall's presence. James and the crew sped off after that, doing wheelies and revving their engines.

Roland did most of his robbing in the South Ward, downtown and sometimes North Newark, but he planned on expanding his range after today

"Now what? We can't do him. That's terrible!" Ivan explained.

"Man, he should have thought about that before he came through my block showing off!"

"Ro, the dude threw me touchdowns and knows who we both are. Chill!"

"See, that mentality right there is why I always tell you, you not built for this," Roland stated.

"Stick to running routes and catching passes." Roland ended the conversation.

By that moment, Mr. Marshall had finally reached the three of them.

"What's going on, fellas?" Mr. Marshall asked.

"Nothing much," they all replied.

Ivan and Lefty grabbed their crates and left the two to talk.

"Did you see that boy last night?" Mr. Marshall asked.

"Who, Dirk?" Roland replied.

"Yeah."

Mr. Marshall was referring to the Dallas Mavericks basketball star, Dirk Nowitzki.

"Boy, did he put on a show," Mr. Marshall said. "The NBA needs stuff like that though, son."

"What you mean, Mr. Marshall?" Roland wondered.

"You don't need one race dominating an entire sport, no matter the race," he suggested.

"For business reasons and for social reasons," Mr. Marshall went on. "Every non-black kid around the world can look and say, 'Wow, I can dominate a sport that I'm the minority in.'"

"That's what made Tiger Woods so special in golf. I wish a black or Hispanic hockey player dominated their sport. There's a sense of parity and equality, you know? I don't want anyone thinking there's a black sport or white sport, so good for Dirk," Mr. Marshall concluded.

Roland took a minute to digest all of what Mr. Marshall had said.

"Yeah, I agree," Roland answered.

Roland would never let Mr. Marshall know when he disagreed with his assertions. He would always say he agreed when he shared the same sentiments, but he would say, "Yeah, I hear you" when he disagreed with Marshall's statements. That was just a sign of how much he respected him.

"Let me know if you have time for a game of chess tomorrow, Roland," Mr. Marshall added.

"Yes, sir. I should be free," Roland replied.

"Okay, be safe," Mr. Marshall said.

In Newark, people would rarely say "see you later," as "be safe" was more appropriate.

"Call me if you need me," Roland insisted.

Roland and Mr. Marshall would end their conversations the same way every time, and neither man would listen to the other's request. Roland never was out being safe, and Mr. Marshall never called him.

With Mr. Marshall gone, and Lefty and Ivan walking back toward the barbershop, it was time to finish their conversation.

"So I want that bike," Roland declared. "I want all those bikes."

"What the hell you gone do with twelve bikes, Ro?" Lefty attempted to laugh the idea off.

"We just need three, the rest we'll flip," Roland implied. "I know a dude who'll pay a lot for them."

"Okay, but you know they'll never come back this way after today," Lefty mentioned.

"Cool, we'll go to them," Roland responded.

Roland was great at planning and executing in the streets. He was a wise general for his age. Many wished he would have used those skills toward something more positive, like his brother, Sean, did.

*

While Roland was plotting on pulling off a new robbery, Sean was in his freshmen year at Rutgers. Tall, dark and blessed with an incredible smile, Sean could light up a room.

He was undeclared about his major at the time, but he had a passion for storytelling. Sean enjoyed writing and watching documentaries. His hopes were to write documentaries about some of the working class people he met when he was a child.

Unlike Ivan, Sean couldn't afford to stay on campus and didn't have a scholarship. He would commute from his aunt's house on the days he had class. Sean had friends but, for the most part, stayed to himself. He was always in the library, as he was once told by Mr. Marshall that the library would be his best friend. The library was a place of quiet and offered all the resources he needed to succeed.

One day Sean came into the library and sat in his usual spot next to the window at the last computer. He was doing some last minute work on a project that was to be submitted online by midnight. It was just a normal night at the library. The usual people were in attendance: the loud football players barely doing work, the older couple who were just using the free computers, and a few study groups of students.

The only thing that was quite different was the presence of females sitting behind Sean. He had recognized one of the girls from one of his business classes. Her name was Sara. She was a very loud, but very intelligent, young lady, who sat right next to Sean in class. Sean had never seen her in the library before. And he had never seen the female she was with before, either.

Sara was sharing a computer with a friend of hers, and the two young women seemed to be struggling to get the computer to come on.

"Hi, Sean," Sara said.

"Hey, Sara. What's up?" Sean asked.

"Nothing much. Do you know how to get this thing to turn back on? My friend was working on her paper, and she thinks it might not have saved," she wondered.

Sean hesitated, as he wasn't an expert in computer operations and he would simply go fetch the librarian for any issues he ran into with the computer. However, Sean didn't want to come off as dismissive, so he made an attempt to help.

"Let me check it out," he mumbled as he got up.

Sean was now standing a foot away from the two young ladies. He couldn't help but notice how beautiful Sara's friend was. Her honey-brown eyes, beautiful smooth skin, and perfectly laid hair were breathtaking.

Sean tried clicking the mouse and pressing buttons on the keyboard, but the computer was unresponsive. He then pressed the power button on the monitor, but he still got nothing. He then quickly glanced to his left and right to see if he saw the librarian walking by. Sean's last attempt was to see if the computer was even plugged in. He got down on his knees in a pair of Roland's old jeans and looked under the table. He immediately noticed that the computer wasn't connected to the power outlet. Rather than tell the two, he smiled, plugged it in and proceeded to act like he was trying to turn it on.

"I know what the problem is, the power supply and PGA Card were off track," Sean lied.

"So now what?" Sara wondered.

“Nothing. All I got to do is press the monitor three times, and then turn this nob twice, and wallah!” Sean explained.

The computer began to load up as Sean held back laughter.

“Oh wow!” Sara yelled. “Thank you, Sean.”

“You’re welcome,” Sean stated as he began to walk back to his seat.

“Wait, how rude of me?” Sara shrieked. “This is my friend, Angel.”

At that point, Angel was gazing at Sean. She smiled, showing a perfect row of pearly white teeth.

“Thank you so much, and my paper did save,” Angel uttered.

“No problem. Do you go to Rutgers too?” he asked.

“Yes, I’m in my final year, thank God.”

“Oh really? Good for you. I’m just a freshman,” Sean noted.

“I’m sure I’ll see you around, Sean.”

“Yeah, I hope so,” Sean mumbled.

Sean had finally headed back to his seat. Unsure if he said the right or wrong thing to Angel.

Several hours had passed, and most of the students including Angel and Sara had left. Even the librarian had headed home, leaving a student-worker in charge. It was 1:00 a.m., and Sean had finally submitted his ten-page paper. His professor would certainly dock a few points, being that the assignment was sent late. Sean always procrastinated when it came to doing things, but daydreaming about Angel definitely caused him to submit the work late.

With his work out of the way, Sean was now headed to the

train station to go home. Sean caught the train the nights he would stay late at the library and missed a ride with Ivan back up to Newark. Sean took the same way to the station every night. On the walk he came across several guys at the train station. The guys were pretending to fight with each other and were talking about beating someone up.

"Man, I hit him like this," one of the guys said.

"Bruh, shut the hell up! You ain't do shit," the biggest one said.

"Who is that?" one of the voices asked.

It was dark near the tracks, and the crew stood under the only light. Sean walked toward the light as he recognized the boys. He recognized that they were all members of the football team.

"Who you?" one of the guys asked.

Before Sean could reply, the largest man interrupted.

"Mind your business, he's good," he declared.

"What's up?" Sean said as he shook the big man's hand.

While the guys may have seen Sean on campus before, Sean knew that the only reasons they didn't bother him was because they knew he was friends with Ivan, but even more so, he was the younger brother of Roland.

By the end of the handshake, the train horn had sounded. Sean boarded the arriving train and headed north for Newark. Sean nearly overslept on the ride back home. He got off the train and had a few blocks to walk to get to his aunt's place. Sean finally reached the house.

Walking up on the porch, he could smell a strong smell of alcohol. Roland and Lefty were sitting on the porch.

"Damn, Ro, why it smells so strong?" Sean asked.

"Man, I spilled half my Yack on the porch," Roland stated. "You want some?"

Roland held up a pint of Hennessy and two red plastic cups.

"Na, I'm good, bra," Sean answered.

"Okay."

"Lefty, you drunk too?" Sean asked.

"Na, he just high as hell," Roland interrupted.

The three all laughed.

"I'm going in to sleep, Ro," Sean said.

"Okay … you going to the game Saturday?" Roland asked.

"Yeah," Sean replied.

"Okay, you can roll with me, then."

Sean paused. Sean knew that he wanted to go to the game, but he wasn't sure if he wanted to go with his brother and Lefty. There were pros and cons to going out with Roland.

"Okay, count me in then," Sean decided.

"Goodnight, little bro. Love you," Roland said.

"Love you too," Sean replied.

4
LAW AND ORDER

The city had more than just an armed robbery plague on its hands. Police officers were under a lot of public pressure over the past two years. A handful of controversial rulings in favor of law enforcement officers involved in police brutality and racial inequality occurrences had left the city uneasy. Every law enforcer was receiving criticism, no matter their ethnicity.

White police officers were hated and targeted by nearly every minority in Newark. Non-white officers felt another pressure as well—the pressure of representing an entire race of people while they balanced their duty to work alongside their fellow officers. No officer felt this pressure more than Louis Little.

Officer Little was a rookie on the force. He was the oldest of two, and his mother was Puerto Rican while his father was

Black. His brown skin and soft hair pissed the white officers off from the very first day they laid eyes on him.

"What the fuck!" yelled Louis.

Louis slammed his locker shut, after seeing a pair of bananas inside it.

"So, who's the comedian?" he asked the entire office.

"Nobody wants to man up and say, huh?" Louis shouted.

There were three white officers, getting dress. No one said anything. It was dead silent, until someone chuckled. The snicker came from another white officer walking into the room. It was four-year veteran Officer Wayne O'Sullivan. O'Sullivan was feared by many but respected by few. Today was his first day returning from a one-month suspension from his misuse of force while arresting a teenage Hispanic boy. O'Sullivan had slammed the boy to the ground, breaking his arm and knocking him unconscious. He had sworn the kid had cursed at him after being told to put out his cigarette in a restaurant. Multiple witnesses had begged to differ.

"Fuck you laughing at, O'Sullivan? You did this shit?" Little asked.

"Is that how you welcome me back, 'Little Lou'?" O'Sullivan replied.

"I see you ain't learn shit since your last incident," Little stated.

"Well, it was hard to dwell on what happened, playing golf and chasing strippers for a whole month," O'Sullivan boasted.

"If I find out you put this in my locker I'm going to—" Little declared.

"Whoa, easy, Little," interrupted Police Captain Ken Finn.

"The only thing you're going to do is head to my office, both of you!"

In a rage Louis headed to the captain's office. Just when he thought his day couldn't get any worse, it did. Captain Finn thought it was a great idea for both Little and O'Sullivan to become partners. The news left Louis speechless. He grabbed his pistol and cap and headed home, since his shift was over.

The whole ride home, Louis thought about how he would undoubtedly have to kill his new partner somehow. As he pulled up to his beautiful home, he noticed his wife's car. Her brand new Audi was freshly washed. Still wet and rims shining with armor oil.

Louis put his Jesus piece around his neck and entered his home to be greeted by his four-year-old daughter, Lina.

"Where's your mommy, baby?" Louis asked.

Lina, his daughter, turned towards the kitchen and pointed. Louis picked her up and headed towards the kitchen.

"Hey, honey," he greeted his wife.

"Hi, love!" his wife, Heather, answered.

Heather, thirty-three, was ten years older than her husband. She was from a well-off family, having grown up in Westfield. Her father had taken years to accept the notion that his beautiful daughter wasn't going to date inside her race. With Heather no longer speaking to him and the birth of his granddaughter, her father had come around to accepting the interracial relationship.

"How was your day?" Heather asked.

"It was okay," he mumbled.

Louis noticed that Heather's mother was in the kitchen also. He said hello quickly. Louis didn't tell his wife, as he didn't want to worry her or seem weak in front of his mother-in-law.

"You sure?" Heather added.

"Yeah ..." Louis replied.

Heather looked at her mom and nodded. Her mother gathered her things and proceeded to leave the house.

"Mom, call me when you get home," Heather stated.

The door had closed behind her mother.

"Have a seat, honey," Heather insisted.

She took his keys from him and began to stroke his back.

"Tell me about it. Who fucked with you?" she demanded.

"Same shit, baby. Same as last week, and last month," Louis complained. "These bastards fucking hate me, I swear!"

"You can't control the way somebody feels about you, and you can't worry about things you can't control," she declared.

"That hate they have in their hearts for you has been there for years and won't just go away overnight, baby," Heather went on.

Louis just sat there, taking in all of what she said.

"Now, get clean so we can eat."

Heather meant the world to Louis. She was his mentor, counselor and body guard if need be. Heather was what they called a ride or die.

*

It was finally Saturday, and the football game was kicking off in an hour. Ro was still asleep. There was a knock on Sean's window. The only people who came through the backyard and knocked on the window were Lefty and Ivan.

Sean opened the curtains, and Lefty gestured to him to open the back door.

"What's good?" Lefty asked as he shook hands with Sean.

"Shit," Sean replied.

"Where this nigga at?" Lefty yelled.

"Still asleep. Hungover from last night, of course," Sean explained.

Lefty entered Roland's room. Roland would never lock his door, as he wanted to make sure that Sean or his aunt could always come in the room and wake him up if they had to. The guys always found it funny to play pranks on someone while they were sleep. Roland was the person who always did the pranking, but he was about to be on the wrong end of the joke today.

"Yooo, Sean, go get the hot sauce." Lefty snickered.

Sean ran and got the hot sauce, as he couldn't wait to finally see Roland get what he had coming to him. Sean passed Lefty the tabasco sauce as he fought back tears of laughter. Lefty quietly opened the bottle as he tiptoed to the head of the bed. Lefty leaned in, sweat nearly dripping off his forehead onto a sleeping Roland. Roland's mouth was slightly open, in prime position. Lefty poured three drops of the hot sauce into Roland's mouth.

Lefty and Sean, both, with tears in their eyes, fought back their laughter once more.

To their surprise, Roland didn't flinch. Lefty leaned in and gave the bottle a couple more shakes, and suddenly Roland's eyes jolted open.

"Oh shit!" the two pranksters yelled.

"I'm gone kick both y'all asses," Roland shrieked as he jumped up.

Lefty and Sean both ran for the bathroom. They just made it in time, locking the door immediately as Roland banged on the door furiously.

"Y'all got to come out sooner or later," Ro ordered.

After ten minutes of laughing and apologizing, the two had finally come out of the bathroom. By then, Roland was halfway dressed and ready to head to the game. He had decided to deal with them another time and just be the butt of the joke today.

"Yo, we pre-gaming now or what?" Roland asked.

Sean just shook his head, as he was amazed that Roland was still talking about drinking more as he was just drinking all night.

"Na, I'm good," Sean replied.

"I'm gone smoke this first, then I'll drink with you," Lefty said.

After a quick session of smoking and drinking, the three were ready to head to the game. The three guys had just entered the stadium when the national anthem began to play. As everyone else stood in silence, caps off and hands across their hearts, the trio walked to their seats, laughing with their hats still on.

"Show some respect!" one of the fans yelled.

The group burst out laughing as Roland waved his middle finger towards the predominately white crowd. They had finally found seats. The crowd was electric, and Ivan was off to a great start, catching four out of the first five passes. This was a big game versus their conference rivals, West Virginia.

The three were sitting watching the game when a guy named Polo came to sit with them. Polo was always looking for Lefty, looking to cop some weed off him.

"What's good, fellas?" Polo asked.

"Same thing," Lefty replied.

"You got anything on you?" Polo asked.

"Yeah, after the game. It's too hot right now," Lefty answered.

"Cool," Polo responded.

The four guys began to watch the game. Their attention began to focus on one of the coaches, tight end coach Gene Bowers. Coach Bowers was very animated on the sideline, yelling at his players and cursing.

"Yo, Polo, didn't you say Bowers was sweet?" Lefty chuckled.

"Sure is!" Polo declared as he walked off.

Roland and Sean both looked at Lefty in disbelieve that a coach on a football team would be a homosexual.

"Yeah, man." Lefty laughed. "And y'all know Polo would know," he joked, referring to Polo being openly gay.

The game had ended in Rutgers getting beat badly, despite Ivan having another great game. With Sean headed home, Roland and Lefty waited in the gym for Ivan to come out of the locker room. The two sat in the weight room, trying to talk to every attractive looking female that walked by.

"There he go," Lefty pointed.

Ivan was walking toward the two when Coach Bowers stopped him abruptly.

"Hey, Ivan, keep your head up! I know you're down about the loss," Coach Bowers whispered.

"Yeah," Ivan mumbled.

"Hey, man, if you're not doing anything some Sundays stop by the park. I got a new kid's team and could use some help," Coach Bowers encouraged.

"Uh, I don't know about coaching, coach," Ivan chuckled.

"Na, man, it will be cool. The kids look up to older players like you," Coach Bowers explained. "Especially someone NFL bound like yourself."

"Alright, coach. I'll let you know," Ivan replied.

Ivan continued to walk over to Roland and Lefty, with his head down, appearing to be taking the loss really hard. The three young men walked out of the building before speaking to each other.

"Nigga!" Lefty yelled.

The three men all burst into laughter, shaking hands and hitting each other.

"Bro, I was killing they asses," Ivan explained.

"They tried to single cover your boy first half, and that was laughable," Ivan continued.

"Bro, you were putting a hurting on the double team too," Roland commented.

Without the team's knowledge, Ivan could care less if they won or lost. His only concern was whether or not he himself played well.

"How many touchdowns the team have?" Lefty jokingly asked.

"Two," Ivan replied.

"And how many you have??" Lefty hollered.

"Two!" Ivan yelled.

The three laughed all the way back to Ivan's car.

"What's the wave tonight?" Ivan asked Roland.

"I just got a text about a house party not far from the crib," Roland replied.

"So we in there?" Ivan asked.

"Yeah," Roland replied.

The crew started heading to Ivan's home so he could change his clothes. While he got dressed, the other two started drinking. One of Ivan's coaches had bought him a bottle of Cîroc a week ago, and tonight was the night they would open it.

The three were all dressed, drank and had a ten-minute drive to the party. They all had on tan Timberland boots, blue jeans and white tee shirts. As they approached the party, they could hear sirens ringing loudly. The house was taped off, and police cars were everywhere. The young lady who texted

Roland about the party walked up to the car.

"Yo, what happened?" Roland asked.

"The boys from across town that be having all those dirt bikes came to the party, and one of them got shot, and they took his bike. He'll live though."

The three in the car looked at each other and shook their heads.

"Who did it?" Roland asked.

"It was Mo. They all from Irvington, but you ain't hear that from me," the young lady replied.

The young lady was Linda, one of Roland's old classmates. She'd always known Roland to be a gangster. Linda had witnessed him commit several crimes and figured that he would let her in on the cut this go around. The worst offense Roland was rumored to have done was the shooting of a competitor. Roland had approached him one night and had given him two options: to get off his turf by the end of the week or the man's kid would grow up fatherless. The man must have taken Roland for a joke, as he had laughed at the threat except he shouldn't have, since he had been shot ten times while driving with his three-year-old child. One summer night, an unidentified gunman had approached the rear right window. He had reached inside the vehicle, quickly removing the baby, shot the man while holding the child, and then placed the toddler back inside the vehicle.

Many had assumed Roland was responsible for the murder, but with the lack of evidence and cameras in the area, nothing had been done. Neighbors said that the police never truly pursued the case, as the man "had it coming to him."

"Mo? ... okay, you go home, Linda," Roland replied.

The three turned the car around and started heading back home.

"Damn, somebody got James' ass before we did, and they shot him," Ivan said.

5

STRENGTH IS IN THE NAME

Officer Louis Little threw his sweet, diluted coffee out the window and buckled his seat belt as Officer Wayne O'Sullivan stepped on the gas.

"Let's get us something, Little Lou, we got action!" O'Sullivan yelled as he turned the sirens on.

The partners got a call from Weequahic High School about a bunch of kids getting ready to fight. The officers were the first to arrive at the location. Half of the kids dispersed as soon as the cop car pulled up. The other half, still arguing, pulled their shirts off, waiting to throw punches with one another.

"Look at these savages," O'Sullivan said.

Louis ignored the comment as he got out the car. Wayne wasted no time, drawing his weapon.

"Y'all better get from round' here!" Wayne ordered.

"What are you doing? Why do you have your weapon out?" Louis questioned.

"Shit, you don't know what these animals are thinking, Little," Wayne mumbled.

The kids all took off running in fear, except one.

"Gone, get!" Wayne continued.

"Move along, young man," Louis urged the kid who looked to be about thirteen years old.

The kid did not flinch. He stood there just staring at the officers. His eyes locked with Officer O'Sullivan's.

"Well, look at this one! This little sum' bitch got a pair on him don't he, Louie?" Wayne declared.

"Boy, you retarded or something?" Wayne asked.

"Fuck you," the youngster replied.

The two officers looked at each other. With his weapon still drawn, Officer O'Sullivan looked around to see who was watching.

"You know what this is, you little shit?" Wayne uttered as he raised his gun.

"Better yet, do you know who I am?" he continued.

"Hey, let's go," Louis stated.

"I'm yo daddy, I'm yo momma, I'm yo mother fuckin' everything," O'Sullivan explained as he placed the cold pistol on the boy's head.

There was a pause. It felt liked it lasted for an eternity, but in reality, it was just five seconds. They locked eyes. Neither gave an inch to the other.

"Yo, we're done here!" Louis yelled as he pulled at Wayne's arm.

Officer O'Sullivan finally lowered his weapon. The two cops proceeded to their vehicle. As they pulled off, Wayne looked at the young kid one more time. To his dismay, the kid raised his right arm with his fist balled up, with a smirk on his face.

"That shit cannot happen again, ever," Louis hollered.

"You're right, Louie, relax, just having a little fun with the fucker."

"And what was that shit about being his father and everything?"

"Oh I meant that shit." Wayne laughed. "Here have a drink, loosen up." Wayne pulled into a parking lot.

"Na, I'm good."

"What kind of cop don't drink?"

"I drink. I just don't drink while I'm on fucking duty. And I don't like beer that much. It makes me feel bloated.

"It's Stella. This shit doesn't bloat you." Wayne chuckled. "And don't say bloat, sound like you talking about your monthly or some shit"

Wayne was on his third beer by the time Louis finally gave in.

"Fuck it, pass me one."

"There you go, let your balls drop, Sweet Lou!" Wayne passed him a beer.

The two spent the last few hours of their shift drinking in the parking lot of Fox's Bar.

"Yo … Wayne … yo!" Louis yelled as he shook a sleeping Wayne.

"What? What?" Wayne shouted.

"Drop me off at home," Louis said.

It was after one in the morning by the time the two arrived at Louis's home. Louis stumbled to his door before making it in. Heather wasn't home yet. Louis assumed that she probably was at her mother's or out with her friends. Lina wasn't home either, since she was staying the night at her grandmother's house.

Louis' stomach rumbled. He went to the freezer and took out some of the frozen pizzas and put them in the oven. He then went and sat on the couch. With his head spinning, he tried to watch a few sports highlights. It was three minutes into the program, and he was now getting a headache. Louis decided to close his eyes.

Forty-five minutes had gone by before Louis finally re-opened his eyes from his drunken slumber. To his surprise, Heather was standing in front of the TV with a pan in her hand with a burnt pizza on it.

"Hey, baby," Louis muttered.

"Thank God I showed up before you burnt the damn house down," she said angrily.

"I'm sorry …" Louis stated. Before he could finish his statement, Louis began to vomit.

"Damn it, Lou," Heather screamed.

Heather began to clean up the mess and got Louis out of

his uniform. She put away his pistol and covered him up with a warm blanket.

"Damn rookie," she said, smirking and shaking her head.

*

The winds were whipping past Sean's face as he walked from the student center on campus. He had a hotdog in one hand and a folder full of papers in the other. Sean had just met with two of the career advisors regarding an internship. He was beginning to get frustrated with the entire process of finding an internship in his field.

Sean put his headphones in his ears as he waited for the train back home. He boarded the train, and to his dismay, it was packed and all the seats were taken. Sean shook his head in frustration and turned his music up.

Two stops later, a seat was finally available. Sean took the seat and closed his eyes. The train made another stop. To Sean's surprise Angel boarded the crowded train. He recognized her as the girl he was introduced to at the library. They both made eye contact and started to smile immediately.

"Here, have my seat," Sean said.

"No, it's okay. You look tired yourself," Angel replied.

"Well, I guess, we'll both stand, then," Sean stated as he stood up.

The two laughed.

"So, what was that 'you look tired, and you look like shit' comment you slipped in?" Sean joked.

"No, not like that." Angel laughed. "You were literally asleep."

"Sleep? ... maybe I was just praying or saying grace!" Sean added.

Both Sean and Angel laughed and joked the entire ride.

"So, where you headed, if you don't mind me asking?" Sean asked.

"To work, well, my internship," she answered.

"Nice, where at?" he responded

"Bill's car dealership, some secretary job that was looking for a pretty face who spoke proper English."

"Cool, how do you like that?"

"I don't, but it pays pretty well."

"I'm looking for an internship and, no offense, I'm not trying to settle for something that don't make me happy. … That's how you waste time you can't get back."

"So it sounds like the search hasn't been going well."

"Na, it hasn't. This career advisor has been suggesting all these internships not in my field. A bunch of shit I'm not interested in," Sean uttered.

"Wow, I see."

Sean noticed his stop was coming up. "I got to go. It's my stop. Good seeing you, Angel."

"Good seeing you too," she replied.

As Sean headed for the train door, he heard Angel's voice.

"Hey, Sean, I have this knack at finding other people jobs. Do you have your resume on you?" she asked.

"Yeah," he replied, handing her a resume out of the folder.

"I'll be in touch," she answered as the train doors closed.

The New Jersey transit train had finally arrived at Sean's stop. He walked a couple blocks up and was home. He reached into the mailbox and grabbed the envelopes inside. Sean walked into the house and threw all the mail on his aunt's bed. His aunt Michelle handled all the bills and Sean's mail. Roland didn't have anything in his name, so he barely received anything.

*

It had been two days since Roland's plan to rob James was altered. Roland was outside in the backyard working out. He had spent his dirty money on a gym set a couple months back. Lefty was spotting Roland while he racked the weights back on the bench.

"What up, bro?" Roland said, smiling. "When you gonna start lifting with your big bro?" Roland asked Sean.

"Next time," Sean asserted playfully.

"Man, Sean ain't messing with no weights," Lefty chimed in.

"Man, shut up," Sean replied.

Sean and Lefty often bickered back and forth. The two were the same age, and they were once classmates, until Lefty dropped out. It always seemed like Lefty was competing with Sean for Roland's attention.

"Where's Aunty?" Sean asked.

"Probably at the mall, I don't know, nigga." Roland laughed as he finished his last set.

"True," Sean replied.

"Yeah, I don't know where she's getting the money from," Roland went on.

"Uhh, she goes to work," Sean responded. He turned his attention to Lefty. "Fuck you looking at, Lefty? You high?" Sean asked.

"You know it," Lefty replied, smiling.

Lefty took out his cell phone and began to take a picture of him and Roland to post on his social media account.

"Yo, what should be the caption for this?" Lefty asked.

"Put 'I rather be famous than rich,'" Roland said sarcastically.

Roland swiftly pressed the delete button on Lefty's phone, erasing their photo.

Roland himself did not have any social media accounts and believed they were for attention seekers and pitfalls.

The three all laughed, shaking their heads.

"Yo, put your shirt on bro, come with me to make this sell really quick," Lefty stated.

"Bitch, I don't need no shirt in my hood," Roland replied.

"Then just come like that," Lefty went on.

Roland looked at Sean's face.

"Yo, Lefty, you go ahead. I'll catch up to you," Roland said.

"Same spot, right?" Roland asked.

Lefty paused, staring at Roland.

"Yeah ..." Lefty answered as he grabbed his top.

While Lefty walked off to sell weed, the two brothers had a chance to talk. Roland recognized that there was something going on with his younger brother.

"What's good with you?" Roland asked.

"What you mean?" Sean answered.

"Your face looks like something's up," Roland went on.

"Man, just this internship and job thing … some bullshit," Sean asserted.

"Bro, you'll find something. You'll get a bunch of no's, but all it takes is just one yes," Roland replied.

While the two were talking, Lefty had finally met his client outside the barbershop. It was the same thirteen-year-old boy who wouldn't leave when Officer O'Sullivan and Officer Little saw him outside the high school.

"Ramadan, what's crackin'?" Lefty said.

"What up? I just need two," Ramadan responded.

"Bet," Lefty said.

"Where's Ro?" Ramadan asked.

"Uhhh … there he go now," Lefty answered.

Roland was walking toward the two. Shirtless, veins and muscles seemingly popping out of every part of his body. The youngster just stared at Roland in admiration and awe. He never met Roland before, but he (like all his peers) knew who Roland was and would pretend to be him on the playground.

"Lil' man just asked about you, bra," Lefty said.

"Oh yeah? What up?" Roland wondered.

The two shook hands.

"This my lil nigga Ramadan," Lefty stated.

"Remember when that teacher got arrested for having them

eighth graders sticking up banks and gas stations and shit?" Lefty chuckled.

"This the teacher?" Roland joked.

"My boy Ramadan played a major role in that shit," Lefty continued.

The two just stared at each other. After a few seconds Roland finally broke the silence.

"You remind me of somebody, lil' man," Roland stated. "But I'll be back, yo."

Roland headed back to the house, checking his phone for missed messages. He got back to the front steps of the house and noticed the door was cracked open. Confused, Roland reached for his pistol, not realizing he had left it inside while he was working out. He eased his way up to the door and peaked in. He never knew Sean to leave the door open, so this worried him. He pushed the door open and walked to the first room. A woman stood in the middle of the living room, holding a child. They both turned towards Roland.

"Daddy!" the little girl screamed.

6

THE TRUTH RELEASED

"Finish your food, baby," Roland said to his three-year-old daughter.

"I didn't know you were coming this way," Roland said to Elizabeth.

Elizabeth Henry was the mother of his only child, Roxanne. Mom and daughter both shared a similar appearance, having caramel skin and long braids. She had two other kids from two other men as well.

"Yeah I know. Sometimes I like to pop up on you," she said.

"I don't know why. Nothing I do should concern you," he replied. "So, what's up? You leaving Roxy for the weekend?"

"Nope, I got her grandmother to watch her, but she does need money."

"Oh, she need some money," Roland asked as he looked at Sean, shaking his head.

"Tell me what she need, and I'll just get it," he added.

"Na, you don't know what to get, just give me the money, and I'll get it!" she yelled.

"… Yeah, you can leave. You ain't getting shit," Roland replied.

The two began to argue so loudly Roxy began to cry. Sean came to her, picking her up and telling her everything would be okay.

"Come on, baby, let's go. Your daddy ain't shit!" Elizabeth continued.

"Don't poison her mind with that shit, bitch!" Roland yelled.

Elizabeth opened the front door with the baby in her arms.

"You black bastard, I don't know why I waste my time asking for help from you!"

"If you weren't the mother of my daughter I would have shot— "

Sean closed the door, interrupting his irate brother. He stared at Roland. The two stood in silence for a couple minutes before Roland broke the silence.

"My bad, bro," Roland said.

"No, fuck that," Sean yelled. "Y'all are going to kill one another. You are going to seriously hurt that girl and go to jail behind that bullshit, Roland!

And Roxy don't need to be around that mess. You don't know the effect that has on a child."

"Yeah I know, bro. She just takes me to a certain place," Roland explained with tears in his eyes.

Both Sean and Roland went to their rooms and closed their doors.

Roland lay down on his bed. He looked at a picture of him and Poppa on his dresser. He took a deep breath and closed his eyes. He knew what he said was wrong, but he wasn't willing to call her and apologize for it.

The front door opened, and Aunt Michelle walked in. She had her hair pulled back in a ponytail, trying to keep cool from the ninety-degree weather.

She didn't see either one of her nephews. She knocked on Sean's door, and when she entered, she could feel the tension.

"What's going on?" she asked as she set down her briefcase.

"Nothing," Sean answered.

"A typical Sean answer. Why am I not surprised?" she said sarcastically.

Sean cracked a smile.

"Is it him?" she inquired as she pointed in the direction of Roland's room. Over time she began to assume that Roland started most of the trouble around the house.

"I'm just tired of it all, honestly," Sean mumbled with his head down.

"Well, you know, I felt that way as well once. Right around your age," Aunt Michelle admitted.

Sean's aunt shared a story with him. She revealed that she understood that he was at the age where he wanted his own.

His own space, his own rules and his own career path. She understood because she could relate. She struggled living under Poppa's roof, abiding by his rules and being forced to deal with the troubles that her family brought along.

"What I would encourage is that you take chances now. Pursue that career. Do what you love. And eventually it will make you money, Sean," she advised as she turned Sean's fan on. "That's what I did. I like helping people. Especially the youth and the elderly. So I made a living out of it. I was so good at helping people that I started making money from it."

Aunt Michelle went on to explain to Sean that the fact that he didn't have any kids or any bills yet meant it was the perfect time for him to take chances—chances that a couple years from now he might not be able to take.

While Sean didn't say much during the conversation, he did appreciate it.

As she got off his bed and walked toward the door, Sean interrupted her. "Can you leave the door open?"

"Sure," she replied.

Aunt Michelle took two steps toward the kitchen when she turned back toward Sean.

"I'm proud of you. And you know who else would be proud of you if they were here?"

"Who?"

"Poppa."

Sean lifted his head and couldn't help but smile.

You could hear Roland's door close after that statement.

Roland overheard the tail end of the conversation. His aunt never once mentioned 'Poppa would be proud' to him before.

Sean, checked his phone, and to his surprise, he had a text message from an unsaved number. The message read, "Hey, this is Angel."

It had been three days since Angel and Sean first started texting. It had started off with her sending him different websites to help land an internship in his field of study, but by now their conversations had heated up. Today they were headed on their first date.

He saved the number.

"I can't believe we stayed up until five in the morning talking about a whole lot of nothing last night," Angel joked as she walked towards Sean up his aunt's walkway.

"I know, that was all you," Sean said as he reached in for a hug.

The two embraced each other, hugging and ending up with Sean gently placing a kiss on Angel's cheek. The two stared at each other for a few seconds before awkwardly looking away from one another. It was clear that the two liked each other, but it was the beginning stages, and both parties were hesitant.

The two were headed to get ice cream from a spot that Angel was familiar with.

"I got family over there at that house," Angel pointed.

It was a beautifully built home that couldn't be more than two years old.

"Wow, I remember living in a big house … well, not that nice, but it was big," Sean said.

"Well the ice cream place is right around the corner. Come on," Angel said as she reached for Sean's hand for the first time.

The two walked into the ice cream parlor where they were greeted by Mr. Marshall.

"Hey, Mr. Marshall. What are you doing way over here?" Sean asked.

"I've been coming to Larry's Ice Cream parlor since before you were born," Mr. Marshall declared.

"And you walked here?" Sean asked.

"Of course, exercise keeps you young.

I know a woman whose coworkers would ask her how she stayed in such great shape, and she simply explained that instead of taking the elevator, she took the steps." He paused to give Sean some time to think about what he just said.

"And that's how life is. Sometimes you have to take the steps and not the elevator to get where you need to be." He turned his attention to Angel. "And who is this young lady here, Sean?"

"Oh, this is my friend Angel," Sean stated.

Mr. Marshall and Angel shook hands. The older man held her hand for a few seconds, staring at her.

"And where have we met before, young lady?" Mr. Marshall asked.

"Forgive me, but I don't recall, sir," Angel explained.

"Hmmm … It'll come to me, I'm sure." Mr. Marshall chuckled.

Mr. Marshall finally released Angel's hand. He gathered what was left of his ice cream and walked out of the parlor. He shook his head as he walked past a house for sale with a foreclosure sign next door to the parlor and thought about his friend Fred and his family who'd sacrificed so much and still had fallen behind.

"That wasn't weird at all," Sean said sarcastically.

The two stayed in the ice cream shop for an hour, talking and laughing.

"So I took a look at your resume and made a few changes on it," Angel said as she pulled out her laptop.

The two stared at the document. Sean's eyes were wide open and in awe.

"Wow, this looks so much more professional. Thank you," he stated.

"I've never really had someone take the time out to help me like this. You should really stop."

"No, I get it. It can be hard if you've never had someone show you how things are done," Angel explained. "And as a black man, you have to be that much better than your competition."

Sean just stared at Angel with a slight smirk. Angel's beauty was no match for her spirit.

"Wow, you're deep," Sean said.

The two both burst out in laughter as they finished their ice cream.

"And you almost didn't introduce me to the older man," Angel said. "I'd had to take away major points from you." Angel laughed as they walked past the same house for sale with a foreclosure sign next door to the parlor, but it didn't catch their eye at all.

*

There were just a few days left in the summer, so Officer Louis thought. He kissed his wife and daughter like every morning after breakfast, put on his uniform and headed out to his car. He passed several homes with foreclosure signs, and although he and his family weren't really feeling the effects themselves, he knew his wife had friends who were falling way behind. He felt pissed off about the crisis. He felt secure, but his thoughts drifted off to how the neighborhoods were changing and work. Louis was so busy and caught up with thoughts about his work, he didn't even realize he missed two phone calls from his mother and sister.

Rather than calling his relatives back, he called his partner, Officer O'Sullivan.

"How far are you from headquarters?" Louis asked.

"Damn, no good morning or nothing, my brother?!" O'Sullivan joked.

"What's up, man? Sure, good morning."

"Meet me down here at Fox's."

"Na, man, no way you drinking at 6 a.m."

"Shit, Little, just come down here."

Louis closed his phone and headed down to the bar. Louis was about two blocks from the bar before he unknowingly ran through a red light while looking at his phone again. He slammed on his brakes just in the nick of time before he ran into the back of an eighteen-wheeler.

"Shit! Fuck! Put the phone down, Lou," he yelled to himself.

Louis pulled over to gather his thoughts. As he took a moment, he heard sirens ringing off from what seemed to be a block away. He checked all his mirrors to see which direction the cop cars could be.

The police dispatcher soon spoke of shots being fired a block away.

"Here we go," Louis said as he sped off.

A ride that took just two minutes felt like thirty minutes for him. Worries of the unknown began to give him a headache. As Louis pulled up to the park, he noticed three police cars already at the scene. Getting out slowly, not really sure what he was getting himself into, he walked to the officers with one hand on his pistol.

Two officers stood over the body of an older male. No one was performing CPR or making any attempts to save the gentleman's life. Louis couldn't help but notice one officer was white, the other was black, and the victim was black as well.

"Uh, uh, what happened?" Louis asked the white cop.

"Routine traffic stop, broken taillight …, Bastard tried to grab my taser, so in self-defense, of course, I, uh, shot him," the officer stated.

Louis stared at the black officer who was wearing blue latex gloves as he had been touching the deceased body.

"That's how it happened, bro?" Louis asked as he glared into the black officer's eyes, seemingly looking into his soul.

"I wasn't at the scene ... officer," retorted the black policeman.

"Hey, don't come down here with that shit, Little! I said that's what happened, so that's what happened!" the white cop yelled as he got within inches of Louis's face.

"Whoa, whoa, whoa," a voice called out. It was Wayne O'Sullivan.

"I heard the call as I waited for you around the corner," Wayne said. "Now let's get out of here. This isn't our fight, kid."

"What's that supposed to mean?" Louis asked.

"It means you can't go around trying to play Doctor King waving your black flag on every corner, son. You have to know when to hold them and when to fold them. Hell, whose side are you on anyway? You're blue now, not black."

Louis looked at Wayne in disbelief and disgust. He looked around noticing that there were several civilians near the park's gate looking on. Louis locked eyes with one particular onlooker. Officer Little walked towards the small crowd.

"Hey! Hey, you!" Louis spoke out to the one man with his phone out.

The guy turned around as if he did not hear Louis and began to walk off.

"Hey, come here," Louis yelled as he took off after the man.

The man didn't get far before Louis had caught up to him.

"Dude, you didn't hear me calling you?"

"No, I didn't," the bystander said.

"Yes, you did. What did you see?!"

"I didn't see anything."

"I think you did. What did you see, sir? I won't hurt you … I'm not like the rest of them," Louis uttered as he looked over his shoulder.

There was a pause. A pause that said more than anything the two had already stated.

"I saw everything," the witness declared.

"Everything?" Louis asked.

"Everything!" the man reassured him.

"What happened?" Louis demanded.

"Take a look for yourself," the man answered as he pulled out his phone.

Louis snatched the phone from the man and immediately played the video. He watched the two-minute and forty-second-long clip. Officer Little was filled with disgust and somewhat joy that what he thought had happened was caught on video. The video was of a black man running away as a white officer fired multiple shots into his back. Shortly after, he was seemingly placing something near the victim, perhaps as a cover up.

The conflict of interest began to set in immediately for Louis. He felt pressure belonging to the minority race to take action, as well as being a sworn police officer. Being part of two distinct groups that seemed to be unable to coexist was no easy matter for the rookie cop.

Louis stared at the man as he held a tight grip on his phone.

"Here, get out of here, and spread that video now!" Louis insisted.

7
THE CAT, MONKEY & CHICKEN

A police cruiser rode past Ivan, Lefty and Roland. It had been a month since The Bulldogs found out Mo had beat them to the dirt bikes.

"And what about the pigs and all these high-tech cameras around town now, that community eye shit?" Ivan said as he looked at the officer eyeing them.

"We at war, fuck those cameras, those gunshot detection systems, man fuck all that shit," Roland said as he looked around his neighborhood and then back at his troops.

"... In war you have to be strategic. We'll work around that."

"It's a lot more police around since this new mayor took over two years ago," Ivan reminded.

"And we'll work around that too," Roland rebutted.

Lefty and Roland looked at Ivan.

"They don't want us here … and we don't want them here. They ran off plenty of hustlers. They ran off a ton of the robbers. Well not me. I'm here to stay. If it's fuck us, then it's fuck them!" Roland said as he flung a piece of paper in the trash.

"Man, I say we kill the mayor's ass. They say he live in the city," Lefty suggested as he lit a Black & Mild cigar.

The two of them looked at him. Laughed. And then pondered the idea.

"Imagine," Roland mumbled.

Little did they know, the police force was having similar conversations. Officers were given similar speeches during their morning meetings. They talked about how they are the enemy when they go into town. And how the gang members and drug dealers wanted to drive them out.

One officer wasn't convinced that they could win the war with the gangs, but the lieutenant assured them that the cops always win.

The gang didn't hold onto the same belief. The people who were trying to provide them some guidance weren't wearing any damn uniforms.

"Yo, remember when Mr. Marshall smacked Ivan with that big ass cane?" Lefty said.

Ivan, Roland and Lefty all began to laugh.

"That shit hurt, fuck y'all," Ivan responded.

"It was all over that sports debate," Lefty added.

"Mr. Marshall asked him why he didn't get into baseball instead of football. He was talking about the money he could make, how physically demanding football is and the difference in career lengths," Roland explained.

"And then Ivan interrupted him and said, 'Man, that shit is boring, and you don't hit the pros until you about twenty-four or twenty-five, fuck that.'" Roland chuckled.

"He cracked you right in the damn head when you said, 'fuck that,'" Roland went on as he laughed.

"I don't know. Maybe we would have played if we had the equipment and enough people," Lefty added.

"Lefty, that was the smartest thing you've said since I've known you," Ivan replied.

The three laughed as they sat on their crates outside the barbershop, smoking and drinking. They just finished bagging up the autumn leaves outside their hangout spot.

All three men had expensive designer outfits. Roland had an all-white Gucci sweat suit on with matching Gucci shoes. Lefty and Ivan both had on Fendi attire. The three young men had about $75,000 worth of jewelry combined on them. The plan was to go to a strip club later that night and blow some money.

The roar of American muscle engines hit Main Street. A purple GT Mustang cruised past the barbershop going about fifteen miles per hour. The car moved slow. Certainly the driver wanted everyone to see who was in it.

Two men sat inside. The passenger was a well-dressed man

named Jerry Campbell. He wore a charcoal Tom Ford Windsor Base Sharkskin three–piece suit. Easily a four-thousand-dollar outfit. Jerry, thirty-six, was easily the biggest drug distributor in Newark. He was accompanied by his brother, David "Doc" Campbell, thirty-four. Doc did all the driving and was the muscle of the two. Doc was 6'5" and 250 pounds. There were stories of Doc throwing men off of buildings that messed with Jerry's money. The two men had been hustling since Roland's uncles were.

Roland's eyes fixated on the men in the car like a cat eyeing a bird in the sky. He had seen the two men in pictures and heard all the stories, but he never spotted them coming through Main Street before.

"Don't even think about it, Ro," Ivan stated as he noticed Roland's gaze.

"I bet them old heads don't think they can get got too," Roland stated as he wiped off his Rolex watch.

"Probably not because nobody has been able to," Ivan added.

"There's a first time for everything," Roland responded.

"Man, you know I'm down if you are, big bro," Lefty uttered as he took a sip of codeine.

Lefty blindly believed in Roland like that. Roland gave him a sense of confidence that was hard to explain.

"We had basically this same talk about them boys with the dirt bikes, and we got beat to the punch with that," Ivan mentioned in an attempt to take their attention off the Campbell brothers.

"True, we got unfinished business," Roland said.

"Who they said got them for those bikes again?" Lefty asked.

"Some nigga from Irvington named Mo," Roland answered as he looked at his phone.

In the midst of the Campbells coming through, Roland missed a collect call from one of his incarcerated uncles.

"Damn, I just sent this dude money," Roland mumbled. "Niggas had money out here and couldn't take care of the family or keep the house, but now they can't stop calling, looking for handouts," Roland announced to his crew.

The three guys sat on their individual crates and finished the last bit of Hennessy, paying no mind to anything else they needed to do. Suddenly, they saw four boys come around the corner. In the front of the small group of high schoolers was Ramadan. Next to him stood a short, very dark-skinned boy. Two feet behind them were twin boys. The siblings wore matching shirts and sneakers. They didn't appear to be trouble, at least for the moment.

"What up?" Ramadan said, speaking to the three sitting on the crates.

The three young men all just nodded their heads.

"This my boys from school, Caesar, Kenny and Kurt," Ramadan said.

All three boys gawked at the expensive sneakers the older gang wore.

"Damn you funny looking," Lefty joked as he fixed his jewelry.

The entire group all began to laugh except Caesar himself.

"I'm playing with you, lil' dude," Lefty said as he reached out, shaking the small dark kid's hand.

"These the boys from your eighth grade class?" Roland asked Ramadan.

"Yeah," Ramadan responded.

Roland, always thinking, had seen an opportunity arise. The plan to have Ramadan and his boys help get the dirt bikes from whoever Mo is had hit him.

"Yo, come inside the barbershop," Roland said to Lefty and Ivan.

"Camp out here real quick," Lefty said to Ramadan as he got off his crate.

The three walked inside the barbershop. They spoke to the barbers, who were all debating with one another about the basketball game on TV. Shouts of Lebron James versus Kobe Bryant rang out.

"Yo, we could probably put these lil' niggas on that Irvington job," Roland stated. "We'll let them know this is their way to prove themselves if they think they gonna be coming around here. I'll slip them a couple dollars from whatever we get for the bikes," he went on. "Shit, I'm tired of always getting my hands dirty," Roland concluded.

"I don't know, man. They're kind of young. Plus, we don't even know how this Mo dude get down," Ivan said.

"Man, them lil soldiers were handling their own in the eighth grade. They can get those damn bikes," Lefty stated.

"Okay, let's just feel them out first," Roland said as he walked back outside. "Yo, all y'all come back by here tomorrow night. We gone watch the Roy Jones Jr fight."

*

"So, Sean, how did the interview go?" Angel asked him as she sat on the porch outside his home.

It had been a month since their ice cream date. The two spoke or met every day. Their chemistry twirled lovely like the chocolate and vanilla ice cream that they enjoyed.

"Felt good, but we'll see," Sean replied. "They said I'll know within twenty-four hours."

"That's good," she answered.

Sean had mixed emotions about the internship position he had put in for at Sirius Satellite Radio. He felt he put forth impressive interviews, but having been declined his last four positions, he was second-guessing himself.

"Well you know what?" Angel asked.

"What?"

"I say we take a shot of this because I'm sure you got it!" she offered as she pulled out a bottle of tequila from her bag.

"Well, I don't know about that but sure," he countered.

"You have to claim it, Sean, speak it into existence," Angel declared.

Sean smiled. Knowing that he had another person who believed in him was reassuring.

The two sat on the porch, laughing and drinking for hours. A car pulled up to the front of the house. It was Sean's aunt Michelle. Michelle knew Sean drank, but out of respect, he put the bottle behind his back out of her view.

"Hey, Sean," Aunt Michelle said.

"Hey, Aunty," he replied.

"Come help me with these bags," she called out as she opened the car trunk.

Sean got up and jogged over to his aunt's car. Sean grabbed all of the bags, making sure he didn't have to make a second trip.

"Not those bags, just the grocery ones." She reached for the bags full of new clothes. Michelle was always well-dressed, having a well-paying job and understanding how important her appearance was.

"And who is this?" Aunt Michelle said as she smiled in Angel's direction.

"This is my friend Angel," Sean explained.

The two women embraced one another to Sean's surprise. Sean had been with girls before, but this was the first time he'd brought a female to his home. Sean quickly carried the plastic bags inside before he lost his grip. His aunt Michelle went inside and closed the door behind her. Just when Sean thought the introductions were over, he heard a loud bang.

The back screen door slammed. That very moment, Sean closed his eyes, wishing that he had taken Angel inside or she had been gone by now. Sean could hear the voices of Ivan, Lefty and Roland coming up the driveway towards him. Sean wasn't worried about Roland's introduction but more so his two friends, especially if they were intoxicated as usual.

"What's good, bro?" Roland said.

"What's good, Ro?" Sean replied.

"This is Angel. Angel this is my brother, Roland," Sean said as he smiled.

The two shook hands. Roland just half-heartedly smiled, not sure what to make of Angel or the potential relationship just yet. Roland wasn't sure if she was just a one-night stand or someone his younger brother was taking serious.

"Oh shit, playa. Ivan, look. This nigga got a chick over here," Lefty yelled. "And to think we started getting worried about you," Lefty joked.

"Fuck off," Sean replied as he stood up.

"Man, I'm playing," Lefty said as the two young men stood face to face.

"Imma make y'all kiss and make up," Roland interrupted, breaking the tension. "We going to the chicken shack. Y'all want something?"

"Yeah," Sean replied.

"No, I have to be heading home in a few. Thank you though," Angel answered.

Sean looked at Angel. Not sure if she meant it or just felt uncomfortable and was ready to go. Shortly after the three drove off, Sean and Angel grabbed their cups and headed for the train station.

By the time the three had got to the chicken shack, the club had let out. All the hustlers and club regulars packed inside the food spot. Roland opened the door that an unaware customer was leaning on. The man nearly fell out the store.

"Who the f—" the stumbling man said.

"Oh, what's going on, Ro," the man reacted as Roland just stared at him.

Roland and Lefty walked past the man and cut all the way to the front of the crowded line, while Ivan stood near the door. Half of the people in line either looked away or left before placing their orders.

Roland ordered food for all three of them. He then looked at everyone, making sure nobody had an issue with him skipping the line. In the crowd one face stood out to Roland. The man's face looked disgruntled as he clearly fought back his comments.

A woman stood next to him. She squeezed his hand and whispered to him, "Don't say nothing."

"Don't say what?" Lefty interrupted as he approached the couple.

Roland just looked on.

"What could he possibly say?" Lefty asked as he grabbed the woman's hand and pressed it against his pistol underneath his shirt.

"Let's just go!" she ordered.

"No, fuck that! These punks could have waited in line like all of us!" the man declared.

Lefty looked at Roland with a sinister smirk on his face. He threw back his dreads and pulled out his pistol, causing the crowd to scatter and leaving the couple and the three men the only ones left in the store.

"Yo, chill!" Roland said.

The man was no longer combative. His hands were in the air as the woman screamed, as if he had been shot already.

"Yo, you scaring this bitch," Ivan yelled.

"Chill out," Roland said again.

Lefty finally snapped out of it, putting his gun away and snickering.

"How much I owe you?" Roland asked the cashier. He threw the money on the counter. "Use the change to pay for their food too." Roland looked at the couple.

Lefty looked at Roland with confusion. The three walked out of the chicken shack to the car.

"Yo, you do unnecessary shit," Roland yelled as he pointed his finger in Lefty's face.

"Man, I was playing, damn," Lefty argued as he smacked Roland's finger down.

"Play like that when I'm not around," Roland stated.

"Man, shut the fuck up," Lefty yelled.

Roland, without saying another word, landed a punch to Lefty's chest that one could hear a block away.

"Who the fuck you talking to?" Roland said.

Lefty crumbled to one knee, gasping for air. Two seconds later he bounced up and went after Roland, swinging with all his might.

"Yo, chill the fuck out. Y'all done made this night hot enough," Ivan announced as he got in between the two brawlers.

"You need to save that energy for them niggas up in Irvington tomorrow," Roland said.

The three men all got in the car. Sitting in silence. Lefty just stared at the back of Roland's head. He felt like he had let Roland punk him. Any other person he would have harmed, but he loved and slightly feared Roland, so he was forced to take the loss tonight. Roland sat in that same silence. He rubbed the back of his right hand, trying to ease the pain from punching Lefty. Despite delivering the better blow, he was still furious. Ivan, turned the music up, in an attempt to break the awkward silence in the vehicle.

"Yo, let's ride up there and scope out that area," Roland said.

The three men sped off to see where Mo hung at. They were three blocks into the town before they started to hear dirt bikes buzzing.

"You got to be shitting me. This is going to be a lay-up," Roland voiced. "Fall back and follow that one." He pointed.

Lefty sat in the back seat quietly. He usually didn't say much after they fought. The one biker led them to another biker, who then led them to a house full of bikes.

"Look at this shit! These niggas out here with them bikes like their shit don't stink," Roland said.

"I still don't see James' bike though," Ivan noted.

"Oh yeah, the one I'm keeping." Roland chuckled calmly.

Like magic, the electric black bike was being rolled out of

the garage. The three sat in the car, two houses down from the gang watching. A female with a bandana on her head dressed in predominately male clothes pushed the bike. With her neck covered in tattoos, she nearly looked like a man.

"Yo, let me call Linda real quick," Roland said.

He would never text anything regarding criminal activity. Roland was smart and knew not to leave a paper trail.

"Linda, what's up? That Mo character you told me about the other night, what he look like?"

"He? Mo is a girl," Linda clarified chidingly.

8

LIFE HAS ITS SPEED BUMPS

"You haven't touched your brew, what's your problem?" Officer O'Sullivan asked.

Louis just stared at the beer shaking his head.

"What you want, some Hennessy? Black people love Hennessy," Wayne joked.

The two chuckled.

"I hope you're not still thinking about that shit from earlier?" O'Sullivan questioned.

"That shit?! A man got shot in his back running away, and you want to stay silent and make a toast to that?" Louis voiced loudly.

"Listen, I got enough on my plate. I'm not looking to add any more."

"At least you got a plate! Man got shot in his back running away today, Wayne."

"Little Louis, I'm a brew away from telling you about yourself!" Wayne said angrily.

"You know what? Chug that beer, and speak your mind!" Louis replied aggressively.

The two officers locked eyes inside their favorite bar. Wayne grabbed the pint of beer and drank it in seconds.

"Okay," Wayne said slamming the pint. "Let me tell you something. You and your people think that y'all are the only ones that grew up poor and have to struggle," Wayne declared. "You think I didn't struggle to get jobs? You think some of us didn't go to sleep hungry some nights? You think I never went inside the hood and been scared out of my mind, not knowing what was going to happen in a community where everyone hated me just because of my skin and uniform?" he continued, and as he did, his voice got louder and more tense.

"You think I don't hear fuckers calling me cracker and shit like that, holding what some ancestors or other cops have done against me? I'm the minority when I show up to work!" Wayne spat out. "You think all of us have it made? Like I'm not wrestling with a divorce and have four kids with one 'son' that's darker than you?" Wayne shared.

Louis just stared at Wayne. The two men just sat in silence for seconds before Wayne got up and grabbed his jacket.

"I think I've said enough tonight," Wayne said as he threw money on the counter.

Louis just looked at Wayne, still taking in all that he said. "Yo, you good to drive?" Louis asked.

"Yup," Wayne replied.

Officer O'Sullivan walked out the door with his head down as Louis finally took a sip of his beer.

"Hey, can I get a double shot of Hennessy and another Corona?" Louis asked the waitress.

As Louis ordered, the bar door reopened. In walked Wayne again.

"How did you know he was running away?" Wayne wondered.

"What?" Louis replied.

"You said the man was running away and got shot in his back. How did you know that?"

There was a pause. Both men realized that they had said too much tonight. Louis rose out of his seat and walked closer to Wayne.

"There's a video of the shit today. A man recorded the whole thing!" Louis whispered.

"And … tell me you destroyed that phone! That video will make all of us look bad!" Wayne continued.

"Man, fuck that! I don't care anymore! The truth is more important than some oath," Louis declared.

Wayne stepped back. He took a look at how serious Louis was, and then his eyes turned toward Louis' line of drinks.

"You know what? You are a real-life super hero," Wayne uttered as he pat Louis on the shoulder. "Let's just start off fresh tomorrow and act like this never happened," Wayne stated as he walked out.

Louis sat back in his seat. Starting with the double shot of alcohol, he began to drink alone.

Louis was six shots and three beers in by the time the waitress asked him how he was getting home. Louis took out his phone and showed her a picture of his wife, Heather, and stated she would come get him if need be.

"I'm good. I'm not even drunk," Louis explained to the waitress.

Louis staggered up and headed out to his car after leaving a big tip. He walked across the parking lot, trying to put his key in two different cars that he thought were his. After he finally found his vehicle, he sat in the driver side and dialed Heather's number.

The phone went straight to voicemail. Louis looked at himself in the mirror, wiping his face of sweat and fixing his curly head of hair. He got out of the car and started to pee in the lot. Louis got back in the car and started the engine. He drove off, taking the same way he'd taken hundreds of time. He was sure that he knew where he was going and was good to drive. He passed several boarded-up homes. His vision was clear, and he was alert.

It was three blocks before the alcohol hit him again. Louis was slowly blacking out as he fell asleep. His eyes were heavy, and his stomach was turning. He rolled down the window and turned up the music to stay awake. Even listening to rappers Jay Z and Young Jeezy could barely keep him awake.

Louis was just a few blocks away from home, stopped at a

traffic light. Minutes later, he opened his eyes, realizing that he was sitting at a green light. He pulled over. He ripped his door opened and began to vomit. Brown vomit dripped on the side of his cruiser. He slammed the door shut and sped off, rushing home before his condition got any worse.

Louis's vehicle bent the corner, shooting through a yellow light. Officer Little was easily going twenty miles per hour, before he struck something in the middle of the road. It sounded like thunder had crashed through the hood of his car. He pulled over to investigate the matter.

When he got out of the car and looked five yards down the road, his eyes no longer heavy, he found himself staring at a young lady's body covered in blood. Her big curly hair covered half of her freckled face. Her petite frame lay lifeless. His heart beat like a drum. He knelt down, seemingly sinking into the ground. Grabbing at his baseball cap and punching at his own face, he stood broken and in disbelief.

Louis looked around and quickly got back in his car. He drove off in a hurry, steering around the woman. He ran a red light as he looked back and forth, checking his mirrors. The rookie officer was now a block away from the bystander, as time felt like it was moving in slow motion. He paid attention to every street sign, every road marking, all stuff he glossed over before this moment. He drove fast but cautious. He was frantic, but did not want to attract attention. Thoughts raced through his head. Thoughts of his wife, daughter, mother, sister and career all went through his head. Guilt filled his heart followed by disgust. How could he leave that woman like that?

After he hooked a sharp U-Turn and darted back towards the incident, he pulled up next to the unconscious woman. No one was nearby, and still the woman had not moved a muscle. He took three deep breaths to calm himself. His heart still seemingly beating through his chest. In a monotone voice, he prayed she was still alive. Louis felt for a pulse. He bent down and picked the lady up in one swoop. He placed her in the back seat, covering his shirt and car with bright red blood.

Before he took off again, he opened his phone and called the only person he could at the moment, Wayne O'Sullivan.

9

BLOOD & KIN

Wayne's phone rang as he buckled his pants, leaving the VIP room of a local go-go bar. His stomach hung over his belt from all the beer. He stared at the phone as the name "Little Lou" flashed. On the final ring, Wayne decided to answer.

"Yeah … now what?" Wayne answered.

"Wayne! Where are you … where are you?" Louis yelled in a panic.

"Calm down! What the hell is wrong with you?" Wayne responded.

"Come to, uhhh, 973 Kittle Court near Richard Lane now!" Louis yelled before hanging up.

"If this is some fucking prank …" Wayne uttered.

Wayne spun his tires as he raced over to the location. He was about ten minutes away from Louis. He pulled behind Louis's vehicle that was parked in a dark alley. Louis stood outside of his car, waving to his partner franticly.

"Turn off your lights! Turn off your lights!" Louis said, waving frantically.

"What the hell is the meaning of all this?" Wayne stated as he slammed his car door.

"I'll show you," Louis replied as he opened his back seat door.

Officer O'Sullivan came closer, staring into Louis's eyes. He knew that it was serious. Wayne looked into the car and was floored at the sight.

"What the hell happened here?"

"I just ran her over."

"How the hell you do that?"

"How I do that? This bastard ..." Louis mocked.

"Alright, alright, calm down! Is she alive?"

"I got a faint pulse a few minutes ago. How long do you think it will take for an EMT to get out here?"

"EMT? What the hell are you thinking?" Wayne declared. "You know what? If you don't need your career or don't mind not seeing your family again, then you go right ahead and make that call, ... but I'm getting the hell out of here!"

Louis just stared at Wayne in confusion.

"If she's dead, then there's no need for you to take your own life as well. And if she's not, someone will see her on the road and get her to your EMT!" Wayne said.

"You know what?" Louis asked.

"What?" Wayne replied.

"Maybe you're right," Louis wondered.

Wayne looked at Louis in surprise, shocked that he would even consider leaving the woman.

"Na, man, that's not right. I don't know. I don't fucking know," Louis re-tracked.

As the two stood there with the door open, they both simultaneously noticed the young woman's chest move. Suddenly, she was inhaling and exhaling. Her eyes jolted open as she took a tremendously deep breath.

"Oh my God!" Wayne mumbled.

The woman reached out in Louis's direction and whispered, "What happened?"

*

Meanwhile, Roland was gearing up for action.

"Yeah, tonight's the night," Roland said to Ivan and Lefty.

All three of the crew—Sean and two of the barbers—were in the shop late at night. The barbershop was full of hookah smoke, and everyone had a cup of their favorite alcohol in hand. The Roy Jones Jr versus Joe Calzaghe fight was just beginning when there was a knock on the glass.

It was the eighth graders. Ramadan, Caesar and the twins all walked in. With the twins grinning ear-to-ear, Ramadan shook Roland's hand first, while Caesar shook Lefty's. Caesar and the twins lined up where the drinks were being poured, in hopes of getting a free cup.

"They know tonight's the night?" Roland whispered to Lefty.

"Yeah, I told them earlier," Lefty replied

"Earlier? You should've waited," Roland said.

"They didn't say nothing to anyone, right?" Roland continued.

"I don't think so, Ro. Na, they didn't," Lefty responded.

"You don't think so or you don't know?" Roland asked.

"Bro, they're good. We're good," Lefty replied as he tapped Roland on his chest.

"Ight, don't let them drink too much," Roland said.

The fight was in the eleventh round, and Roland still had not gotten a call from Linda. Linda was to give Roland the drop on Mo and the bikes, as she was at the fight party in Irvington at Mo's.

"Yo, anything?" Ivan asked as he sat next to Roland.

"Brrrr, na," Roland replied.

Roland wasn't worried. After all the things he's been through, he always had faith that things would work out in his favor.

"Yo! You gonna text ol' girl!?" Lefty yelled across the room.

Roland just looked at Lefty angrily.

"My bad," Lefty followed.

Just as he finished his statement, Roland's phone rang. It was Linda. Roland got up and walked outside the shop so no one could hear his conversation.

"What's up? Tell me something good," Roland said, answering the phone.

"Hey, so everybody in here is pretty drunk off their asses. There's about three to four bikes here and a bunch of other shit like laptops, TVs, all kinds of games, and phones, man," Linda explained.

"Wow, how many shooters? Any guns?"

"Hard to tell. Probably about six of them that's here for that. … The rest will run as soon as you pull up," she explained.

"And where's my hoe, Mo?" Roland chuckled.

"Mo is here on the couch with two girls all over her, one of them taking pictures posing with Mo's guns. … some real groupie shit."

"Guns? That's plural?" Roland demanded clarification.

"Yeah …" Linda declared.

"Okay, say no more. You get out of there now," Roland uttered.

Just as Roland hung up his phone, a cop cruiser rode by. The officer rode past, staring at the legendary stickup kid. Roland stared back and just shook his head. While cops were aware of who he was, he knew that he was "clean," and they couldn't take him down for anything as of now.

Perhaps, the biggest factor into why Roland had not been charged with any major crime was the fact that he had laid a blanket of fear over the neighborhood. No one would testify against him in fear of retaliation. Victims either never made it to court or they stopped appearing out of fear.

Roland walked back into the barbershop with a sinister smirk on his face. Ivan, Lefty and Sean knew that look. It was *go time.* Sean started to head home. The other two threw away their cups and rallied up the youngsters.

All four of the young thugs walked toward the car they showed up in. Caesar pulled out a yellow screwdriver as he got inside the driver side of the car. A couple tries at the ignition, and he had got it started up again. Roland, Ivan and Lefty were all driving in a rental that Ivan's Coach Bowers put in his name for the football star.

The plan was simple. Caesar, the driver, would park on the street behind Mo's trap house in Irvington near Chancellor Avenue and Stuyvesant Avenue. Ramadan and the twins were going to go through the backyard, enter the garage and take the bikes. Everyone was said to be inside, as the boxing match was still going on. Caesar would stay in the car just in case someone had to make a run back. Ivan, the other driver, along with Roland and Lefty, would wait out front, a few houses down. Roland and Lefty would go in shortly after the younger crew to make sure they got out smoothly.

Both cars were in position. Ivan, Roland and Lefty parked out front a few houses down, while the eighth graders were parked on the street behind Mo's house. Little did Roland know, Caesar and Ramadan had changed roles.

Caesar had begged Ramadan to switch spots with him, as he wanted to get in on the action and not play lookout from the car. Ramadan had finally given in to Caesar's persistence, vowing that if the plan did not go right because of the switch, Roland would be done with them.

Caesar and the twins got out the car. They all held pistols and wore black ski masks and gloves. They crept over the fence and tiptoed through the backyard. The three approached the garage door. Bolting into action, they pushed it open with their weapons drawn. They quickly located three dirt bikes being covered by blankets. They were all chained up to the garage. The three needed to find a key to the padlock or something to cut the chain.

While the three were rambling around in the garage, there was another issue unfolding. Linda had made a mistake. Linda was about a block away when she realized she had left her phone at Mo's house. The twenty-year-old, turned around quickly and headed back to the house.

Linda's heart raced as she hurried back. She got to the house within a couple minutes. She walked across the grass and opened the door. Without her knowledge, Roland could see her entering the house.

"Shit, yo, why the hell Linda go back? I told her to leave," Roland said out loud.

"Bro, call her," Lefty suggested.

"What? Nigga, hell no! I'm not calling her while this is all going on," Roland responded.

Meanwhile, Caesar had finally found a bolt-cutter to break the chains off the bikes. The three unloosened the chains and started hauling the bikes out of the garage. Rather than quietly push the bikes, Caesar started them. The twins followed his lead. All three engines roared loudly.

One could hear the bikes being turned on from the second floor of Mo's trap house.

"Wait, who's on the bikes?" Mo asked out loud. "Somebody, go check."

Just as Caesar and the twins were about to ride past the house, the side door swung open. Two of Mo's shooters came barreling out.

"Who the fuck are y'all?" one gangster yelled.

"Uh, we the pizza boys," Caesar stated as he aimed his gun towards the men.

Caesar let off three shots from his .22 caliber pistol, causing the men to jump behind a parked car in the driveway. The twins gassed their bikes down the driveway while their friend kept shooting. As they shot down the hill, both of the boys took out their phones on queue, seemingly recording the heist.

Just as Caesar began to try and make a dash behind the twins, the two marksmen began shooting back.

Roland and Lefty both got out of the car once they heard all the shooting. Their masks and gloves covered them as they walked the dark street. By the time Roland and Lefty got up to the house, Caesar had ducked behind a car with the bike. The thirteen-year-old was all out of bullets and faced three of Mo's men.

Mo looked out her window. She would have had a clear shot at Caesar if he wasn't slouched behind one of the parked cars. She went to the other window where she noticed something odd. She noticed a parked unfamiliar car.

After wondering where the thieves could have come from, she had a clue. She quickly went downstairs and jogged toward the stationary vehicle. She cut through her backyard and jumped over the fence. She pulled out one of her guns, leaving the other tucked in her pants.

Mo crept around the back of the running car. The car windows were slightly tinted, but she could tell there was someone inside. She raised her Beretta, and by the time the unaware Ramadan noticed her, it was too late. Mo fired one shot, striking the thirteen-year-old in the face. His head lay on the car horn, alerting the neighbors. She placed the firearm to her side and ran away from the car before firing again.

Meanwhile, Roland and Lefty had managed to back Mo's guys inside the house. They fired several shots at the men, striking one in the shoulder. The men fired back from inside the house, trading shots with Roland and Lefty.

Both Lefty and Roland slid behind the car Caesar was hiding behind.

"Yo! You good?" Lefty asked Caesar.

"Yeah," Caesar replied.

"Where's the other bike?" Roland asked. "The black one."

"I don't know man. We grabbed what we could," Caesar uttered.

"Y'all get out of here," Roland told the two.

"What, bro? Leave that bike," Lefty urged.

"I'm good. Trust me," Roland replied.

Roland and Lefty did their signature gang handshake.

Caesar and Lefty got on the bike and sped off. Roland got up from behind the car and headed to the garage. He aimed his pistol with the red laser dot pointed toward the house in case one of Mo's men still wanted to shoot it out.

He opened the garage door, picked up a flashlight, and quickly looked around. He noticed a ladder. He looked to the ceiling and saw a door leading to the roof of the garage. He set up the ladder, quickly climbed it and pushed the door open. He looked back, with his gun pointed toward the door, ensuring he had no followers. Surely, he wasn't going to leave without getting what he came there for in the first place. There it was on the roof—the electric bike. The bike that once belonged to James and then Mo was now his.

Roland quickly picked up the light bike. He managed to get it down the ladder without falling. He got it to the door when he heard women screaming.

Roland opened the door, and to his surprise, Mo was standing outside several yards away. The two locked eyes like two old gunslingers. Both held firearms in hand, but neither were shooting yet. The screams of people inside were too distracting.

"Yo, people got hit," one of Mo's henchmen said.

One girl came crawling out of the house, bleeding from her shoulder. The other girl being carried out had a bullet in her neck. It was Linda. Roland just stared in shock. Mo raised her Beretta toward him. He turned the bike on and darted off before she could get off a shot.

"Y'all take them to the hospital," Mo said.

The gang leader finally put away her gun. Walking through the house, she stepped on empty bullet cases. There had to be about thirty shells inside and outside the house. Blood was everywhere. Mo turned off the TV as the final bell rang in the fight. She sat in her chair shaking her head, thinking about all that just happened. Mo rose and looked out her window again. To make matters worse, the car that she shot the boy in had vanished.

*

Sean and Angel had been officially dating for a couple months now. Their relationship was truly blossoming. They had created a "Love Box." It was an empty shoebox where they stored all of the sweet memories and gifts they exchanged with one another. The two had been going on all kinds of dates, rock climbing, skating, heading to the aquarium, and ice cream runs. This next date would be the most nerve racking for Sean. It was his turn now to go to Angel's home to meet her family for Thanksgiving.

"It will be cool. You'll meet my parents and my brother," Angel explained.

"I've never been to a girl's house … to meet her family," Sean said.

"Are you done in there?" Angel asked from outside the bathroom.

"Yeah, just trying to get this tie on."

"Let me see," Angel uttered as she pushed open the bathroom door.

Sean had his tie in one hand and his phone in the other. He was looking at a "How to Tie a Tie" video online.

"I got you," Angel said as she snatched the tie from Sean, laughing.

"No, I got it," he responded.

Angel took the tie and swooped it around Sean's neck. In three strokes she had the tie perfectly tied around his neck.

"Where'd you learn that from?" Sean asked.

"My last boyfriend," she replied.

The two stared at each other.

"No, silly, my dad and brother. I'm sure your dad or brother showed you before, and you just didn't pay attention," Angel joked.

"I wish that was the case," Sean mumbled.

Angel quickly realized that bringing that topic up had changed the mood in the room. The two never spoke much about Sean's relationship with his father and brother. It was always Sean asking about Angel's family or her volunteering personal information.

"Ready," Sean declared nervously.

Sean drove his Aunt Michelle's new car to Angel's home. His aunt was one of the few people on the block with a car with a top-notch heating and cooling system. Sean didn't feel embarrassed driving it and figured walking from the train wouldn't be a good first impression.

His aunt knew this and wanted Sean to make a good first impression. Loaning her car was something she never did. *But this was for good reason*, she had thought.

He wore a blue dress shirt with the dark blue tie Angel helped him with. Blue jeans and black low top Reeboks to complete his semi-formal look. Angel on the other hand went for a more comfortable look. She wore a bright red Rutgers sweater and Ugg boots to go with her black leggings.

“This is nice. If you don’t mind me asking, what does your aunt do for a living? She always seems to have something new,” Angel questioned as she took off her boots and folded her legs.

“Honestly, I don’t even know. She works in a big fancy building downtown, answering phones for some politician, I think,” Sean answered.

“Yeah, you don’t know,” Angel chuckled.

Both of them laughed.

“Well, whatever she’s doing, she’s doing it well,” Angel stated.

“Yeah,” Sean replied.

The two were quiet.

“I could see if her job is hiring?” Sean went on.

“Uh, na,” Angel replied.

“Na, what? You don’t even like what you’re doing now at the dealer. What you afraid to step outside your comfort zone? You afraid to take a chance?” Sean asked sarcastically.

“Shut up!” Angel answered.

The two laughed again. They had finally pulled up to Angel’s house. There were two nice cars and well-cut grass. Christmas lights and decorations covered the house in the middle of November.

After parking, Sean walked around the car to open Angel's door to her surprise. They began to walk.

"Switch sides. The man is to walk on the outside, closer to traffic," Sean declared.

"I've never heard of that before." Angel laughed.

"What? I'm sure your dad or brother told you before, and you just didn't pay attention," Sean replied.

The two laughed again. They did a lot of that together—teaching each other and laughing together. Just as Angel went to put her key inside the door, it opened. A dark-skinned man opened the door. The man was, Leandro, Angel's father.

"Hey, Dad," Angel said. "This is Sean."

Sean still had the jitters. This was his first time meeting a girl's father and not knowing his own father did not help. Roland never talked to him about situations like this, so this was all completely new.

"And this is my madre, Sandra," Angel said as she hugged a beautiful older Puerto Rican woman.

The two women kissed each other on the cheeks and began speaking Spanish. Angel's mother welcomed Sean with a big hug and kiss on the cheek—a hug Sean expected, but the kiss on the cheek caught him off guard, as it was not as common in his culture. Sean thought Angel's mother was warm and friendly. She offered to take his coat and began preparing his food. Sean was more concerned with impressing her father.

"Hey, you catch any of the basketball game?" Sean asked as he tried to make small talk.

"No, which game?" Angel's dad asked.

"He doesn't really watch sports like that," Angel interrupted him, laughing.

"Oh, okay," Sean replied.

"Well, I do but more so martial arts and boxing sometimes," her dad answered.

Sean wondered to himself, what could he and this older black man have in common. He figured that they both loved Angel, so he decided to talk about her.

"I know you guys have some old pictures of Angel."

"Of course, we do," her father replied.

"She gets a kick out of seeing my baby pictures when she comes over, so this is payback," Sean continued.

"Okay. Well before we do that, let's eat," her father said.

Sean began to fix his plate. Angel interrupted him by holding his hand, as it was time to say grace.

"Let us pray," Angel's mother said.

"Before we eat, we always pray," Angel whispered to Sean.

Sean tried to remember the last time he prayed. He would only say a prayer after something bad happened. As he took in the mix of newness and the nervousness he was experiencing, Sean enjoyed the dinner. Empanadas, Arroz con Pollo, and homemade cookies were all delicious. The whole family laughed and shared pictures all night. Sean and Angel's father talked about current events, Angel and law enforcement, since he was a retired police officer. Leandro spent twelve years as an officer in Hillside before he was hurt in a car accident. He received a lucrative compensation check, being that the incident occurred while he was on duty. The family had seen the accident as a blessing, as the payout had helped provide financial relief and Leandro had had more time to spend raising his children and instilling key life values.

An hour into the visit, the doorbell rang.

"Oh, ese debe ser tu hermano," Angel's mother said: She went to fetch the door. In walked Angel's brother, Lou. A brown-skinned, curly-haired man.

"Hey, Dad," he greeted.

"Hey, Lou," her father replied.

"That's Officer Little to you, sir," Angel's brother, Louis, replied.

"You're right, Officer Little!"

Louis couldn't help thinking about the expression on his father's face. That look of pride seemed to come at Louis so strong, yet, he wondered how often his dad thought about all the stuff that Louis had already seen that disturbed his thoughts. He'd know. Of course, the one expression his dad would hopefully never see or know was the one that Louis couldn't wait to see when he showed up at the hospital later to see the woman he'd hit with the car … if she could even express anything when he arrived.

10

OLD AND NEW WOUNDS

An hour had passed when dinner was over and Officer Louis Little started his car. He drove from his parents' home to University Hospital where the woman he ran over was being treated. He wanted to see how she was doing, and more importantly, see if she remembered what happened the previous night. Louis had taken the woman to the nearest hospital after she woke up.

Memories of the previous night filled his mind as he went to the front desk and checked in as a visitor. He took the elevator to the fourth floor. The officer's baseball cap was pulled down low with a hood on top of that. He got up to the door and knocked. The door opened seconds after his knock. It was a nurse.

"Come on in," the nurse stated.

"Thanks, hey, question," Louis whispered as he stepped backwards.

The nurse stepped forward.

"I'm a close friend. How's she doing?" Louis asked.

"She's doing a little better each hour. She should be free to go tomorrow," the nurse reported.

"Okay, that's all?" Louis asked.

"Yeah, she has a facial fracture, a bunch of bruises and a mild concussion, but she'll live," she explained.

"She'll live … will she remember stuff?" Louis questioned.

"She remembers everything," the nurse said.

Louis stared at the nurse like he had seen a ghost.

"Well, everything up to her accident," she finished.

"Okay, good, well good in the sense she remembers most of what's really important," Louis replied.

The nurse just looked at him.

"You can enter now … close friend," the nurse uttered.

Louis walked in slowly. The TV was on, and the woman was sitting up watching the news. She had a few scrapes and small bandages on her face, but one could still see her beauty.

"Hey," Louis mumbled.

"Hi, Louis it was, right?" the woman replied.

The strangers looked at each other for a split second.

"Yeah, but more importantly, what's your name?" Louis asked.

"Johanna, Jo Jo for short." She chuckled.

"How you feeling today?"

"A little better," Jo Jo declared. "It hurts when I try to remember, though." Jo Jo snickered.

"Don't, then," Louis suggested.

"I, uh, brought you some flowers," Louis went on.

"Oh, you shouldn't have," Jo Jo said as she grinned ear to ear.

The woman stopped and put her hand on her head.

"You okay?"

"Yeah, just the headache," she uttered.

"Well take it easy ..."

Louis's phone rang, interrupting their conversation. It was his wife, Heather. He ignored the call.

"Well if you need anything else, just let me know," he said as he wrote his phone number on a napkin.

"You've done plenty. I can't thank you enough, finding me in the road like that and getting me here ... now flowers. You're an angel," Jo Jo replied.

"Sure, I think I did what anyone would have," Louis replied.

Louis began to head for the door.

"So that's it?" she asked.

"Uh no, you need anything?" Louis asked.

"Na, guess that was just boredom talking ... or this headache."

Louis opened the hospital door and headed out. Before it could shut and lock him out, he came back in.

"Hey, if it's okay, I'll stop by tomorrow," Louis uttered.

"I would like that," she answered with a smirk on her face.

*

"What the fuck happened back there?" Roland yelled as he slammed the door.

Ivan and Lefty just shook their heads in disbelief.

"We had a plan, and them little motherfuckers didn't stick to it!" Roland went on.

"Why was Caesar in the yard and not Ramadan?"

"Man, I don't know," Lefty mumbled.

"You vouched for them, said they were good. What the fuck was I thinking listening to you?" Roland declared.

The three just sat in silence. Lefty sparked up something to smoke, as Roland just looked at him in disgust.

"Linda—" Roland was still trying to process that Linda had gotten shot.

"Yo, Caesar just posted Ramadan is in the hospital," Lefty stated.

"Posted? Why would he have posted some shit like that online?" Roland replied in anger.

There was an awkward silence amongst the gang.

"He got half his face blown off, but he's alive," Lefty jittered.

"That little nigga drove himself to the hospital with a bullet in his face, damn!" Ivan exclaimed.

"He a dog, a dumb dog, but a dog, nonetheless," Roland uttered.

"So, we going up there?" Ivan asked.

"Na … I am," Roland replied.

Roland walked outside, leaving the two behind. He made sure to grab his aunt's car keys off the kitchen table before leaving. Blasting music, he sped off to the hospital where Ramadan was.

He parked outside and walked up to the front desk. Roland was standing in line behind a man with a hat and hood on. He overheard the man say he was "visiting a friend," giving only the patient's first name, and got through. Roland followed suit.

Roland found himself on the elevator again with the man.

"What floor?" the man asked.

"Four," Roland replied.

Roland got off the elevator and headed to the room where Ramadan was said to be. He entered the room without knocking. He walked to the end of the bed and tapped Ramadan's foot.

"You are one ugly mafucker," Roland said, laughing.

Ramadan raised his hand, sticking up his middle finger.

Half of his face was covered in bloody gauzes. He was hooked up to two oxygen machines, but he was in stable condition.

"Yo, how long they trying to keep you here?" Roland asked as he looked over his shoulder.

Ramadan shrugged his shoulders, as he was unsure. He sat up.

"Well, as soon as they say you can go, you need to bounce. There's no telling how long before ol' girl find out you still alive," Roland urged.

"Even if so, she don't know exactly where I'm at …," Ramadan mumbled. The thirteen-year-old coughed up blood before he could carry on his statement.

"What nigga? These streets don't wait to talk, cuz. Well you sit yo ass here and wait for that bitch to come and put a pillow over your face," Roland said.

"I'm out. I left some leftover Chinese food from Fong's for you."

"Thanks, bro," Ramadan said.

"Yo, what do you want to do with your life?" Roland asked.

Ramadan, like a young Roland, was caught off guard by the question, being that no one had ever asked him that before either.

"I don't know," Ramadan stuttered.

"What do you like?" Ro said as he looked at Ramadan.

"Music. I want to be a rapper."

"Seriously?" Ro asked.

A bit of relief came over him, as he was pleased that the young boy had aspirations of more than just shooting and robbing.

"Good, cuz these streets have an expiration date," Roland declared.

By the time Roland got out of the hospital, it was dark outside. He swapped his Aunt's car for his newly acquired bike. He threw Aunt Michelle's keys on the kitchen table and rushed out the door before she could fuss at him. Not only did he not put gas back in the car, he didn't even have the decency to adjust her seat back to the way she had it.

Despite starting a war, Roland went to Fox's to drink. He entered the bar and grabbed a seat, putting his back against the wall.

"Henny and Coke," Roland requested.

"Make that two," a voice said. It was the same man from the hospital Roland had run into.

"Eh, my man, if you call yourself following me … I'm not the one," Roland whispered.

"Oh shit, my man from the hospital. Na it's not like that … pure coincidence," Louis explained.

"I'm Louis," he went on.

"Okay," Roland replied.

"Can I sit here?" Louis asked.

"Go ahead, I'm not staying long," Roland said.

The bartender brought back both guys' drinks.

"Separate tabs?" she asked.

"Yeah …" Roland stated.

"Na, I got this. My man look like he had a long day."

Roland looked on curiously.

Louis pulled out a wad of money and paid for both beverages.

Roland's eyes lit up, seeing the money this guy was carrying.

"Good looking out, but you ain't have to do that," Roland stated.

"Na, man, it's nothing. We ran into each other for a reason. Anyone that go straight from the hospital to the bar could use a free round I'm sure," Louis emphasized and looked up at Roland, employing a nervous laugh and shaking his head sensitively. His father had taught him and Angel about how much easier it was to talk to people who might be on the ropes if you didn't get right in their face but showed interest in whatever they were struggling with.

"That's true," Roland replied.

"Whatever it is, just pray on it," Louis suggested.

Roland just looked at the man. He didn't want to disrespect his beliefs, but he knew the last time he prayed was after learning Poppa died.

"So who were you visiting?" Roland asked.

"Uhhh, a friend," Louis stated.

"You?"

"Yeah … a friend," Roland replied.

The two both laughed. Not giving either man an inch of information.

"So, you out of here," Louis asked.

"Na, I could do another one. This one on me," Roland said as he pulled out his own wad of money.

The two went drink for drink. Both going back and forth, paying for drinks and laughing at people inside the bar.

Toward the end, Roland slowed down on the heavy alcohol. Rather than drink up all of Louis's money, he figured why not just take it.

I just have to get him outside, he thought.

"Yo, you smoke?" Roland asked.

"Na, man, I told my partner to quit that shit too," Louis uttered.

"Partner?" Roland questioned as he wrinkled his face.

"Oh na, I'm an officer, not like that, man." Louis laughed.

"Ohhh," Roland said in disbelief.

Several minutes went by and the small bar began to get crowded as all of the stools began to get taken up. Roland couldn't believe that here he sat, the most notorious robber in the city, throwing back drinks with a cop.

"That's what's up, man," Roland replied.

"What do you do?" Louis asked.

"Man, I do a lot of shit. I'm like a renaissance man or something," Roland stated.

"I respect it," Louis said as the two tapped glasses.

"Yo, if you still wanted to smoke, I think my partner left cigarettes in my car you can have," Louis replied.

"Uhh, na, I'm good, bra. Thanks."

"I have to run," Roland said as he stood up on the sticky floor covered in spilled alcohol.

"Okay cool! Nice meeting you, my man," Louis said goodbye.

"Yeah … it's Roland by the way," he disclosed, feeling that it would be wrong if he didn't at least tell the officer his name, all things considered.

"Roland, I'll see you around."

Roland got on the electric dirt bike and began to ride home. He couldn't stop thinking about his interaction with the police officer. He started to wonder whether or not he said the wrong thing to Louis that would reveal who he was, but the more the alcohol hit him, the more careless he became.

"Man, I don't give a fuck," Roland said out loud as he

stood up on the infamous bike.

Just when his worries began to sink in and make him trip out, he came back to reality, telling himself that he didn't choose this life, he was forced into it. At no point in his young life did he ever want to grow up to be a gangster. He just picked up on what was around him and made the best of his situation, he told himself.

Roland kept thinking of how that cop at the bar had to have a rich family because he didn't know any police officers from his neighborhood. In some weird way, Roland began to become jealous and envy Officer Louis.

Just when his mood began to swing, he reminded himself how he was 'winning'. He popped a wheelie on his newly acquired bike and sped off home.

*

There was a quiet knock at the door. Sean could hear it from his room where he and Angel lay. It was almost unnoticeable. Sean had stayed up all night sending out his application and was trying to avoid getting up. The knock grew to the point it was a full-on bang. Sean finally got up.

"Who is it!?" Sean yelled.

He staggered to the door, wondering who could be knocking like this at 6 a.m.

Sean opened the door. A man stood at his eye level, dark-skinned with a patchy beard. His clothes were stained, and he smelled of alcohol.

"Can I help you?" Sean asked.

The man just stared at Sean. He had a slight grin on his face.

"Uh, my man, I don't know if you're drunk or if you think you know me, but I'm closing the door," Sean stated.

"I know you, alright," the estranged man uttered. "I knew you before you knew yourself," he continued.

Before the two could continue, Roland woke up and dashed to the door. He stood at the door behind Sean. Roland moved Sean out of the way and stared at the man.

"Go back where the hell you came from!" Roland declared.

"Roland..." the man yelled as the door slammed in his face.

"Yo, who the hell was that?" Sean urged.

"A sperm donor," Roland replied as he walked back to his room.

Sean followed Roland.

"Was that our father?" Sean wondered.

"Your father? That nigga ain't shit to me anymore," Roland stated as he climbed back in bed.

"What does he want?" Sean asked.

"I don't know, and more importantly, I don't care," Roland said.

"I know what he doesn't want. He doesn't want to be a dad. So don't go trying to see what he wants," Roland continued.

Sean walked back to his room. He looked out his window where he could see his father sitting on the front porch. The wind blew hard on the coatless man. His father blew inside his hands while rubbing them together, trying to keep warm.

“Everything okay?” Angel mumbled.

“Yeah,” Sean replied.

“You sure?” ahe asked.

“… No,” Sean whispered.

Roland woke back up to voices laughing and food cooking. He grabbed his Walther PPK handgun that rested in between his bed and dresser. It was a small piece that he carried around the house. He walked toward the kitchen.

To his disgust, Sean, his aunt Michelle, and his father were all sitting around the kitchen table. Roland didn’t say anything as he just stared at the three of them.

“Hey, Ro, you see who’s here?” Aunt Michelle asked.

“Yeah, I saw him earlier before I closed the door in his face,” Roland answered.

The room went quiet. Aunt Michelle rarely criticized Roland. She gave up on trying to guide him in life, years ago. She was simply content with the fact that she knew he was alive and could somewhat monitor what he was doing, being in the same household. Her fulfillment to her late sister and father was keeping Roland alive and helping Sean become a productive member of society.

“Son, have a seat,” the man said.

“Cut it out,” Roland said laughing.

“Have a seat …” Roland mimicked him.

“I’m trying not to snap, but what could you possibly want, my man?” Roland asked.

“I’m not your man. I’m your father,” his father replied. “I

came to see y'all," he continued.

"Na, it don't take ten years to get a train ticket," Roland declared.

Sean and Aunt Michelle watched on as the two men went back and forth. This carried on for ten minutes straight.

"Ro, let him speak," Sean demanded.

Roland just stared at his younger brother.

"Go 'head. Speak," Roland said.

"Alright, now there's no excuse to be out of y'all life for this long, but my intentions are good."

"I just want to spend time with you two, as tomorrow isn't promised," he stated.

Roland looked at him, still not convinced at all. He then looked at Sean and his aunt's face, and he could tell they both were open to giving the man a chance.

"Introduce yourself," Roland said.

"To?" his father asked.

"To your baby boy," Roland said sarcastically. "Hell, he saw you this morning and had no clue who you were," he continued.

"You missed that part, Roland, when you stormed off," Aunt Michelle interrupted. She just shook her head, as she was annoyed with Roland's behavior and refused to hold back.

"Na na, Michelle, for your sake, Roland … I'm your old man, Sean, uh, born Richard Webb, thirty-eight years ago. I was sixteen when I had Roland, and four years later I had you. Not proud of it, but I used to sell coke on two blocks. I had two houses at one time and four cars." He chuckled nervously.

He hadn't had to explain himself to anyone in the family ever since Poppa died, and he sure as hell hadn't had any idea how to face all the challenges that came with his sons looking to him for everything. Hell, he hadn't even had it in him to deal with life on life's terms when Poppa had been around, let alone suddenly have to be some sort of father giving them fatherly advice in their lives. He looked at his son, and he hoped his son Sean hadn't saved showing his hardened side for when Roland was looking on. He pictured their mother, always so happy when Sean had curled up in bed with her, like it was the only moment that felt like it was sweet, but the feeling wouldn't last long, he remembered.

"I don't mean to laugh, I guess that's just my nerves," Richard explained.

"I lost all that once we started messing with the coke. Instead of just selling it, we started using it. Typical shit!" Richard said as he shook his head. "We, as in your mother and I. She loved that shit, man. Loved it. I couldn't get her off it after a while. Eventually we lost her," he said with sorrow in his voice. "That woman meant the world to me. She meant the world to you guys too. I couldn't replace her. So, I left y'all here. With your aunt and plenty of money," Richard explained as he looked around the home.

"I had to get away from here. The feds were chasing me, and your mother's ghost was too," he confessed as his voice cracked.

"But today, I'm clean. I drink a little, but who don't … huh, Ro?"

He looked at Roland in hopes of a smile or at least a smirk, but Roland gave him nothing. His face was as stiff as a statue.

"I'm here wanting nothing. I'm here if y'all need anything," he concluded.

"With that said, let's eat," Michelle announced as she stirred the spaghetti.

The three all began to eat, while Roland left the kitchen.

Roland walked to the barbershop where he was to meet Ivan and Lefty. On his way over to the shop, he ran into Mr. Marshall.

"Hey, Roland, I saw your father this morning getting off the train!" Mr. Marshall said.

"Yeah, he came by the house," Roland explained as he looked away.

"You seem upset about that. Na, na, na, son, don't be like that. You can't worry about what someone didn't do for you and what not. Sometimes you have to accept people for who they are. I'm not excusing his absence, but you don't know that man's story either," Mr. Marshall said.

Roland just listened—no rebuttal or response. Despite not wanting to hear Mr. Marshall's statement of acceptance, he knew he was right. Right as usual.

"Quick game?" Mr. Marshall asked.

Roland hesitated.

"Yeah, sure," Roland replied.

The two men sat in two wooden chairs inside the barbershop. Passing neighbors looked through the glass windows as Mr. Marshall pulled out the chess set from inside his bag. They were silent for the first fifteen minutes, each studying the board and smacking their chewing gum. The cool November air suggested he'd be seeing nasty, ugly snow soon greased up by the neighborhood's city vehicles, cop cars and sanitation trucks—all grimed up from all the things people didn't want lying around. He could already feel the grime on his skin like he'd walked out of a meth smoke house.

Mr. Marshall broke the silence.

"Don't you think it's a shame that we don't own more stuff?"

Roland just looked at him.

"All these houses and stores, all owned by other ethnic groups, folks that just came inside our neighborhood and took over," the elderly man said as he moved a piece.

"Yeah, the government designed it that way," Roland said.

"Yeah, partially true, but we also allow it. And you get what you allow," Mr. Marshall said.

Roland moved his knight piece as he listened.

"We'd rather take short cuts. We'd rather sell drugs and rob, rather than work an honest living. Nearly impossible to go to the bank and get a loan as a hustler or stickup kid," Mr. Marshall continued.

"Yeah, I know," Roland answered.

"Your aunt has a job. A good job. And she can sleep at night. Not worrying about the feds or some jokers kicking in her door," the old man said as he moved another piece. "She helps the mayor fight for laws. Laws that you take for granted," he explained. "Let me tell you something, Roland, do you know how many houses have foreclosed and your aunt's is somehow still in your family?"

Roland shrugged, not even paying attention to what other people were struggling with.

"Foreclosures are peaking right now. We're talking one out of every thirteen one-to-four family structures in this city. People are having a hard time, Roland. Lots of us are scrambling. You know who else had an honest living?" Mr. Marshall asked.

"Who?" Roland asked.

"Your grandfather. After retiring as a mechanic, he got into real estate. He owned the old house you guys used to stay at of course, and he owned my old store. He never talked to you about his jobs as a mechanic or how he got into real estate because you boys were too young to understand, but I know he loved learning about how those engines run and don't run. Such a good generous man. He let me run my store rent-free for the final five years."

Roland took his eyes off the board and looked at the older gentlemen.

"He was able to afford the same shit those hustlers, y'all call yourself imitating, could," Mr. Marshall declared.

Roland smiled, reminiscing about the first person he ever looked up to.

"Checkmate," Mr. Marshall said with a grin on his face.

"Damn it!" Roland said.

Usually the chess battles held for longer, but the conversation distracted Roland. Roland was a little upset, as he was extremely competitive.

"I have to meet my guys," Roland excused himself, showing his irritation.

"Alright, son, remember what I said," Mr. Marshall stated.

Roland shook his head up and down.

"You know what to do. You just have to do it," Mr. Marshall said.

"Alright be safe."

"Call me if you need me," Roland replied.

"You know what helps me? Saying a little prayer. Pray on it, Ro," Mr. Marshall stated.

That was the first time they ended their conversation differently. Roland just took in the suggestion of prayer as the old man left.

Roland was feeling upset that he hadn't known what his Poppa had done to get his life in order unlike everything he'd picked up from growing up. He actually was surprised that the thought of asking his aunt had never occurred to him. Poppa just seemed like he was together. Just was. A man who just didn't go right or left every time there was a chance, just solid. And somehow Roland had never even considered how he'd gotten his money, and of course he'd done it honestly. That's why it hurt him so much to think on it.

And what good was prayer for him now? Roland was already

making his money nothin' like Poppa did. Real estate? Being kind to tenants like Mr. Marshall. What was so cool about mechanics anyway? There wasn't a single time Roland had ever fixed a car or a bike, cause when he needed one, well ... Roland stopped the rush of thoughts flying through his mind. He felt his face cringe up, almost like he might cry.

Na, you winning, Ro, don't worry, he told himself. *You winning. Ain't no sense in thinking about all this if it's gonna make it harder for me to get by. I didn't choose this.*

He snapped back into reality again. This life was forced onto him and like he always told himself, he just picked up on what was around him and made the best of his situation. A product of his environment. No sense in praying that he could be more like Poppa anymore.

11
MORE TIME TO SPEND

Sean knew working in politics wasn't for him after having spent a full day earlier this year at the Mayor's office shadowing his aunt Michelle.

"Yes, if not for the Mayor, at least do it for the city that helped raised you," Aunt Michelle said on her cell phone as she pushed through the two glass office doors.

"Hey, Sean, grab that chair and follow me," she whispered as she held her phone away from her face.

Sean grabbed the chair and followed behind his aunt. He looked around the office. It had been years since he'd been inside. Not much had changed. Cream painted walls, carpeted floors and dated bathrooms.

Aunt Michelle was a few steps ahead of him, still on the phone handling business. It was Monday and as usual she had her full suit and heels on. Monday was a big business day at the Mayor's office. The phone lines were swamped to start the week. And with every ring, there was an opportunity to increase revenue.

"Yes, open up your schedule and let's put some time on your calendar to connect. I would love to show you some of the new things we have cooking up in the city," Michelle explained as she paced back and forth in her office.

Sean watched his aunt go on and on. Phone call after phone call. Email after email, scratching and clawing to bring in money for the city. She spent hours explaining how Newark was turning around and on the rise despite what some media outlets portrayed.

"Six colleges and universities, the fifth-busiest airport in the country, a regional transportation system that includes light rail and an Amtrak station, the nation's fourth-largest seaport, and the headquarters of numerous national corporations," Michelle told a potential investor.

Sean watched his aunt in admiration and in disappointment. He had high regard for her passion and enthusiasm. She was quite fierce. Quite the lioness. Simultaneously, he felt like she was begging. Why should a person so educated and successful in her own right be subjected to pleading for money?

"Our mayor inherited a $118 million budget deficit when he was elected. The city of Newark will not be an easy fix, but it will be fixed. And that's only with the help of big name investors like yourself. Think about what it would do for your brand name, once it's announced that you helped turn the town around," she continued as she began making her coffee.

Sean listened to his aunt fight for the city of Newark. His aunt reminded him of the working people he grew up idolizing as a youth. Sean wondered why she cared so much about this poverty and crime-ridden place. He questioned why any of those seemingly honest working people still gave a damn about this city.

Aunt Michelle hung up the phone. For the first time, all day she wasn't on the phone. Sean saw the opportunity to ask her a question.

"If the city is so bad, how come people don't move? How come you don't move?" Sean asked as he unwrapped his lunch. "I know, as soon as I get enough money, I'm leaving."

Michelle got up and closed her office door. She walked over to the window. Her office was seventeen stories high, overlooking the city. She opened the window and called Sean over.

"What do you see?" she asked him.

"Buildings … and … houses," he answered, slightly confused.

"Yes, but I see something even deeper. I see a town full of fighters. I see businesses and homes. I see America and opportunity. There's money flowing through those buildings. Thousands of jobs are being created here to lower the unemployment rate, Sean, but some people overlook that," she said. "And then over there, while you see houses, I see homes. I'll admit, I haven't seen this many boarded up houses in Newark in all my life, but those houses are people's homes and were people's homes before foreclosure hit. Those are homes that have been passed down for generations. Homes that people are willing to fight for. This is our city, son. Yes, you can leave. There's nothing wrong with that, but before you go off fixing on the neighbor's home, make sure yours is intact. Just remember that."

The two looked at one another. Nothing more was said, but everything was understood. Sean heard his aunt loud and clear. Her calling him son triggered thoughts of his own mother. Pleasant thoughts. Images of how she would look and sound if she was alive today filled his head.

Sean was reminded of the choice of flight or fight. To run from his city or help save it.

*

Roland walked over to the barbershop. Ivan and Lefty sat on their crates in silence.

Roland walked inside to say hello to one of the barbers who seemed somehow to be getting by and hadn't lost his home. A television in the back corner reported the news. "Tax-lien sales and mortgage payments and the subprime mortgage crisis aren't easing up on small businesses. Bid rigging of auctioned, tax-liened properties leads to arrests, prosecutions, as the illegal activity harms distressed homeowners."

It seemed like the barber winced for a moment when Roland watched him read. The barbershop had been there for most of

Roland's life. He'd seen every one of the men in his family get haircuts there. He walked back outside, thunderstruck.

"What's good?" Roland asked. Roland could always sense when his troop's morale was low.

"Yo, word around town is the twins been talking about the shit that went down in Irvington for those bikes," Ivan revealed, as aggravated as he'd ever been.

"Oh yeah? That's true, Lefty?" Roland asked.

Rage built up inside of Roland as he tried not to disturb anyone at the barbershop sitting down and talking to each other about health, families, work and what was going on in Newark and in the world. None of that ever concerned Roland. He wondered why they even bothered wasting their time when all they had to show for it was acting like they had it together and wishing they had bikes like he'd recently scored.

"Allegedly they took a video on their phones and have been posting it and showing the shit at school, cuz," Lefty suggested.

Roland just shook his head in disgust.

"So, first, they fuck the plan up, cause a big shoot out, Linda, who I haven't heard from, gets shot, and now they're showing the shit?" Roland said angrily. "Yeah, I got something for they asses, say no more," Roland said.

Roland stormed out the barbershop, slamming the door behind himself. Before he could get far, Ivan was calling him back.

"Yo! Come here, bro," Ivan yelled.

"What?" Roland yelled.

"You not gone believe this shit," Ivan continued as he shook his head.

Roland walked up to the football star.

"Look," Ivan stated as he showed Roland his phone.

"That's the video online. This shit is a news website, bra. We gone get knocked for this shit if they trace this back to us," Ivan explained.

In the video, there was someone on the back of a dirt bike filming and the gun shots being fired at the house where the shootout that left one dead could be heard. Luckily no one's face was in the recording, but Roland still had had enough.

"Yo, I'm gonna fuck them up," Roland declared.

"What you got in mind though, big bro?" Lefty asked.

"Shit, I don't even know how I'm going to handle this, but they gone learn," Roland uttered.

"Have them little niggas come to the shop. I'm about to go get Ramadan out of the hospital," Roland continued.

"Damn, he ready to come home already?" Lefty asked. His surprise at Ramadan's speedy recovery seemed more like a joke because he brought his fingers shaped like a gun to his face and pretended to shoot himself and then proceeded to laugh.

"Yeah, man, the prince is something special," Roland declared.

Lefty just looked at Roland as he walked out of the barbershop. As Roland walked out of the barbershop, an unmarked police cruiser pulled up. Two detectives got out of the vehicle. Both well-dressed, wearing black suits. One of the detectives, white, standing a few inches over six feet, had on black shades. The other was a black man. He was the shorter of the two, but his compact build indicated that he was just as strong as his partner.

"Roland Webb, can we have a word with you?" the white detective asked.

"For what?" Roland replied.

"Just a couple questions," the other detective replied.

"Man, I don't know shit about shit," Roland uttered as he continued to walk away.

"You're a person of interest in a shooting," the detective stated.

Roland continued to walk. He kept telling himself to "play it cool," despite his mind beginning to race about what shooting they could be talking about.

"Man, y'all reaching," Roland said.

"Do we look like we're playing?" the detective asked as he touched Roland's arm.

"Man, so how come you ain't cuff me, then?" Roland asked after a pause.

"Just come with us. It already looks funny, you out here talking to detectives, you know," the shaded detective suggested.

Roland looked around. Every neighbor outside or standing on their balcony was staring at them. Thinking about his reputation, Roland walked toward the police vehicle. Just as the detective was closing the back door behind Roland, you could hear a few onlookers applaud and yell, "good riddance!" Hearing that stuck with Roland. That was the first time his community felt safe enough to voice their opinions on him.

The entire ride over to the station, that's all he thought about. He didn't pay attention to the two detectives smirking back and forth at one another, thinking that they had something on him. He didn't think about an alibi. He just thought about how "his people" wanted him gone. However, rather than empathize with them, he grew angry.

He shook his head, mumbling, "I ain't do shit to them. Fuck them."

He thought about the conversation he had with Mr. Marshall, and for some reason that made him wonder, *Maybe they had a reason to want me out of there.* But just as quickly as he began to try to understand his neighbors, he told himself, "Them niggas ain't never help me. Where was they when I needed them?"

The three men had finally arrived to the station. The two detectives walked very close to their person of interest. They had Roland wait inside a room alone for thirty minutes before questioning him. The two detectives walked into the ice-cold room.

"Roland Webb. Man. You are hard to catch up to, you know that?" the detective established.

"Yeah that's because I be working," Roland replied.

The three men paused before bursting out in laugher.

"Cigarette?" one of the detectives offered.

"You know I don't smoke. Y'all been following me for two weeks now," Roland announced.

The detective put away the cigarettes.

"So, cut to the chase," Roland demanded.

The shooting in question was the one that occurred outside Mo's house that left Linda and several injured. Roland kept his cool. He figured that the detectives would try and link him with the twins, if they had seen the video the boys posted. He knew not to volunteer any information or fall for any mind games they might try. He assumed they would say the twins said something about his involvement, but Roland knew it couldn't have been anything strong if at all since he would have been under arrest already.

"You was seen speaking with these young kids," the detective said as he slid the boys' pictures across the cold table.

Roland looked at the photos.

"Yeah, they go to my barbershop … little nappy-headed niggas," Roland joked.

They began to question him about his whereabouts on the day and time of the shootout.

"Do you know this person?" the other detective asked as he showed him a picture of Linda.

"Yeah," Roland said, shaking his head.

"You guys spoke twice the week she was shot. In fact, you were one of the last calls she made," the investigator announced.

"What's up with that?" the other officer added as he played with a pen.

The black detective sat across from Roland, taking notes on a small pad. The other, walked around the room, asking the majority of the questions. Roland was not handcuffed, as the officers wanted him to feel relaxed.

"Man, she's an old class mate. We were just catching up. She liked me," Roland explained.

"Did she seem like her life was endangered?" the taller detective asked.

"Na. And if so, I don't think I would be the person she would have told, as we weren't that close," Roland said, rolling his eyes. "This is a waste of time, I have to go pick up my daughter, sir," Roland said.

"Come on! Word around you got the streets on lock. A couple shootings involving several people you associate with, and you don't have anything to do with it?!" the frustrated investigator said as he slammed his folder on the table.

Roland just stared at the two men.

"Am I under arrest?" Roland asked.

"No," the white interrogator replied.

"Well, fellas, I'll see y'all around town. Stay woke," Roland replied as he stood up out of the uncomfortable chair.

"Hey, there's a witness who saw you out there. You and your crew, Lefty and Ivan. Once I get them to make a statement, and we will, you will wish you had more time to spend with your daughter," the black detective said.

Roland just stood still, listening to the disheartening words. He put on his best poker face to not show that the detective's words got to him. For some reason, the picture of being behind bars and not being able to see his daughter struck a nerve.

Roland walked out of the precinct. He looked to the sky, and snowflakes began to hit his face. Winter was here.

12
FIRED

"Hey, so I was telling my brother, Louis, more about you," Angel said.

"Oh boy, what you say?" Sean questioned.

"Nothing bad, fool, just about your job search," Angel explained.

"What? What did you say?" Sean asked.

"Just said you have been having trouble like most people," Angel responded.

"What the hell? You got me looking like some bum ass nigga. Trouble like everyone? You don't have those issues. You the newest recruiter for BET," Sean uttered.

"Wow, Sean, you have so much pride. And you sound pretty jealous. What's so wrong with what I did?" Angel defended herself.

"Nothing," Sean said.

The two sat quietly inside Angel's home near the fireplace.

"So what did he say?" Sean asked.

"He said, 'look into law enforcement,'" Angel mumbled.

"Law enforcement!?" Sean yelled.

"So, he wants me to be a cop like him. Man, won't nobody speak to my ass ever again if I became a damn fed," Sean stated as he thought about Roland.

"I wouldn't care what other people thought," Angel responded.

"Man, everybody cares about what others think. That's just some shit people say," Sean replied.

"You should be thinking further ahead. Ten and twenty years from now you'll be happy with your decision," she replied.

The two sat there in silence again.

"I was just trying to help. I know not to do that again!" Angel said.

"Na, it is what it is," Sean answered.

"Well, I have to go and pick my mother up," she said.

Angel got up and headed to the front door. The two both walked outside where the snow was still coming down.

"Hey, tell Louis I want to talk to him more about being a cop," Sean mumbled.

Angel smiled. "Okay … I love you," Angel answered.

"I love you too," Sean replied.

*

Meanwhile, Louis's relationship with Jo Jo, the woman he struck with his vehicle, was growing. The two had been in constant contact for about three months now. Louis unknowingly was getting caught up. He would visit her every day in the hospital, all while ignoring phone calls from his wife, Heather. Originally his visits were to ensure that she did not remember what happened that horrific night, but now he was setting up to see her after her hospital release.

Louis pulled up to the coffee shop to meet Jo Jo. She wore her big curly hair out freely and was in her early twenties. She was at the shop waiting for Louis, sitting in a booth alone, stirring a cup of hot chocolate. The young officer had parked around back where few cars were parked. He pulled his cap down low as he walked through the back door.

"Hey, hon," Jo Jo said.

The young lady stood up out of her seat and gave the officer a hug and kiss on the cheek. This was the first time they touched one another. She wore a skin-tight long black dress. He noticed that she had beautiful eyes. It was the first time he really looked at her without his feelings about possibly destroying his entire life coloring the way she looked. She looked calm, beautiful, and he was very attracted to her. He'd found her more and more attractive over the past few weeks, but the lighting in the hospital was a lot worse than this coffee shop. And despite the fact that he felt like he had made sure he looked good for her, he suddenly felt a bit shy and wondered about how he looked to her.

"You, uh, look nice. A bit much for coffee though," Louis said. He thought they were only meeting for a coffee, and he suddenly felt way underdressed.

"I'm going out after this with a couple friends," she explained. She started to regret getting so dressed up, but she didn't want him to keep picturing her in hospital clothes if she was really going to get him interested in her. She calmed herself down. "You look great, Louis!"

"I figure with jeans and a t-shirt what could go wrong?" He looked down and back at her to notice how great she looked despite the effect it had on him momentarily. He let the feeling pass and decided to really enjoy her in that dress. It hugged every curve. *A lot better than what she looked like in that hospital rag*, he reminded himself. He started to relax, although he felt flustered.

"So, where are you from?" He realized he knew nothing about the person sitting across from him.

"Originally from Brooklyn, but I've been living on the edge of Newark for a couple months now," she explained. This was the first time she had to explain her journey to someone before, so she began to get nervous herself.

"I moved out here for work," she said as she blew her hot coffee off.

"A big change?" Louis asked.

"Not much actually. Besides the cost of rent," she replied. The two both laughed. The laugh helped break the awkwardness somewhat. Knowing that they found the same thing to be funny was a slight relief. "What about yourself?"

"I lived in central New Jersey all my life," he answered. He stopped himself from going into any further detail. He still had yet to mention his wife or daughter.

Every time Jo Jo spoke, Louis looked at her lips. He couldn't help but notice, she had nice lips and a perfect smile. A smile that reminded him of someone. His wife. *I should really mention my wife now*, he thought. But he didn't. Why? The two sat inside the small coffee shop for several hours exchanging stories and getting to know each other. For the first time, Louis started to find Jo Jo attractive.

She checked all the boxes of attraction for him. She was funny, they shared similar interest, she was working, beautiful, and family oriented.

They riddled each other with first date type questions like: What do you like to do in your free time? What's your favorite movie? Any pets? Where have you traveled? How many siblings do you have?

Every question except, "Are you married?" But how? Maybe Jo Jo didn't want to know. Maybe she was married herself. For Louis, maybe he didn't want her to know yet, if at all.

"Wow, damn, it's 5:05 p.m. already," Louis said as he looked at his phone.

His phone had three missed calls, one from his partner, Wayne, and two from Heather.

"Um, I have to run," Louis indicated.

"Where you off to?" Jo Jo asked.

"Back to work," he replied.

"What do you do?" she questioned.

"I'm a cop," Louis said.

"Oh, wow! That's hot," Jo Jo responded.

"Yeah, I guess." Louis laughed.

The rookie officer got in his Dodge Charger and sped off.

"Hey, baby, sorry. I was tied up with O'Sullivan," Louis said to his wife on the phone.

While he was on the phone, he heard a beep. He looked at his phone, and it was a text message alert. It was Jo Jo.

"My friends cancelled on me. Want to meet up tonight?" the message read.

Louis stared at his phone before replying.

"Yeah."

*

"Houston, we have a problem," Ramadan slurred.

"Na, Houston, them niggas have a problem," Roland replied.

Roland and Ramadan sat in Roland's backyard after finishing their work out. The snow had cleared up, but it was still brick out, so the guys lifted in their hoodies and thermal shirt. Meanwhile, Ramadan showed Roland a video of the twins being escorted out of class by detectives.

"Them niggas did some bullshit, man. Recording shit. That's why I don't have no social media. You need to delete that shit if you have it as well," Roland ranted.

"I don't have shit. I deleted all that before being released from the hospital," Ramadan mumbled. The teenager's speech was still hindered after being shot in the face by Mo.

"The only people that should be on there is women and people that's chasing their craft, like rappers," Roland explained. "You still got any more of those painkillers the hospital gave you?" Roland asked.

"Yeah, I got a bunch of them. I ain't use them shits. Them shits will fuck you up," Ramadan responded.

"Okay, let me get those," Roland stated.

Ramadan threw Roland a bottle full of painkillers.

"Yo, where the twins at now?" Roland asked.

"I don't know. Want me to text them?" Ramadan asked.

"Na, never text somebody before shit goes down," Roland declared.

Ramadan just looked on. He knew the severity of the situation.

"I can take you where they be at," Ramadan stuttered.

"Bet, let's go," Roland said.

The two got in the car. No Ivan, no Lefty, no anyone. Just them two.

"Yo, I know those your boys from school and all, so if you want to hang back, I get it, but these dudes have to understand that there's rules to every game, and they broke the rules," Roland gave him an out.

"Na, I know," Ramadan replied.

"Okay," Roland said in shock.

Ramadan always impressed him. From the day he met him,

he always saw a younger version of himself. The teen reminded him of when he would follow Blue around before he was incarcerated.

"Yo, crush those pills up and pour them in the vodka," Roland insisted.

Ramadan smashed all of the pills up and poured them into the pint of vodka. The pill mix was invisible.

"Now, pour me and you some of that water there in those red cups," Roland pressed on.

Ramadan did as he was told.

"You know what separates you from the rest? And I mean from all them niggas?" Roland asked.

"What's that?" Ramadan asked.

"You listen. Not just to me but to people and situations," Roland acknowledged.

"It pays to listen," Ramadan claimed.

"It pays to fucking listen!" Roland chuckled as he shook the teen's hand.

The two rode twice past the twins' house, twice past the playground, once past the gym but could not find the boys.

"Where the fuck these little niggas at?" Roland wondered.

"Well, they not at the precinct anymore," Ramadan declared.

"How you know?"

"They posted 'leaving out' and talking some shit thirty minutes ago."

"Word? Them niggas stupid. Let's just head by the barbershop," Roland said.

Roland and Ramadan pulled up to the barbershop, and to their surprise, the teenage twins were inside.

"Get them to come outside. Tell them we got some shit lined up again," Roland explained.

Ramadan hopped out of the car. He jogged up to the shop, waving at people who hadn't seen him in weeks.

"Yo, grab y'all shit. Something came up," Ramadan urged the twins.

"Oh shit, when you get discharged?" Kenny asked.

"We can talk in the car, cuz," Ramadan stressed.

"Hold up. Let me grab my phone," Kurt stated.

Ramadan just looked on in disgust at the twins. The three all got in the car with Roland.

"Y'all want something to drink?" Roland asked as he held up the bottle of vodka mix.

"Na, I'm good," Kurt replied.

"Uh, I'm straight," Kenny answered.

Ramadan looked over at Roland in disbelief.

"It's free ...," Ramadan mumbled.

"Na ...," Roland whispered as he stopped Ramadan in his tracks.

"Yo, so what's poppin?" Kenny asked.

"I came across another hit, similar to the last one we did. I know y'all down," Roland contended as he looked at the two in the rear view mirror.

"Yeah, no doubt," both the twins replied.

Roland pulled up to the back of a newly abandoned house.

On the ride over, he told the twins that there was valuable stuff left behind in the place.

"So look, Ramadan, you wait out in the car. Don't get your ass busted this time, Two Face," Roland joked.

Ro made Ramadan wait outside for two reasons. He knew that he still wasn't one hundred per cent back to full health, but even more so, part of him didn't want to involve the youngster. He didn't want Ramadan to turn out like Lefty did, under his wing.

"Ha ha, real funny. So, twins, y'all gonna go grab shit with Ro," Ramadan said.

The three got out of the car. They all wore something covering their faces. Even though it was dark out, they wanted to make sure no one saw who was entering the vacant home.

"Yo, let's make this quick," Roland declared.

The three of them began to push stuff all in one corner. There was a bike, expensive silverware, wine bottles and furniture.

"We can grab everything except the furniture," Roland instructed as they bagged stuff up.

"Hurry up, Kurt," Kenny said.

"Nigga, you slow," Kurt replied.

"Yo, we need to burn the shit we don't want, so our prints aren't on it," Roland yelled as he began pouring gasoline around the house.

"True, that's smart," Kurt replied.

"Yo, Ro, how you know about this place?" Kenny asked.

"I used to live here," Roland disclosed as he continued to pour gasoline throughout the house.

"What?" Kenny asked.

"Yeah, post this!" Roland declared.

Roland ignited a lighter and threw it to the floor. The entire floor was covered in gasoline, surrounding the twins. The old house caught flames immediately.

"Ro … No!" the boys shouted.

Roland made his way out the back door, closing it behind himself. He stood near the door for a few seconds. He could hear the boys coughing from the smoke. And then he could hear the boys screaming. Screaming, shouting, crying and banging for help. The screams were so loud Roland took off running before the neighbors could realize what was happening.

*

"My sister tells me you want to be a cop," Louis said.

"Yeah, I'm interested in law enforcement or whatever," Sean replied.

"Na, don't refer to it as whatever. It's more serious than that," Louis stated.

The two sat in the backyard of Angel's parent's house playing games and cooking on the grill, while Angel sat inside. Winter was over, and the spring offered a nice day to cook outside.

"Why do you want to join law enforcement though?" Louis asked.

"The pay is good in the long run. Plus, I think I could do a better job than these cops today."

"Now if you go into it like that, they will throw your ass out.

See this police shit is a brotherhood. They'll never welcome someone with that mindset. Thinking you could do a better job than them," Louis declared.

"Yeah, I got you," Sean mumbled.

"Now don't get me wrong, shit ain't perfect, but at the end of the day, we protect each other. We're all the same color when that uniform goes on. Well, at least we're supposed to be," Louis explained. He chuckled after his statement as he thought about his partner and their personal friction.

Louis put away the playing cards and took out the chess set.

"You have to take care of your mind and body. Feed both of those," Louis shared.

"Like I stopped eating meat after watching a documentary. I got these veggie burgers if you want one," Louis continued.

"I never had one before," Sean said.

"Open up those buns. Try one," the rookie officer replied.

"Yo, where you get all this 'take care of your mind and body' stuff from anyway?" Sean asked.

"Nowhere specific. Just stuff my dad always preached, and people who helped raised me, like this older man, Mr. Marshall," Louis replied.

"Mr. Marshall? As in the man who walks everywhere with a cane dropping knowledge all day?" Sean uttered.

"Yeah, you know him, huh?" Louis said as he put out the fire.

"Yeah, all my life," Sean said.

"Small world."

"So, you want to be a cop because you see an opportunity to help your community, and you need financial stability," Louis stated.

Sean looked at Louis blankly as though he wasn't sure the best thing to say yet, so he just listened.

"Okay, so this cop thing is to be taken serious. You can't be in it just for the money or you won't last. What are you good at?" Louis asked.

"Uhhh …," Sean chirped.

"You have to be good at something." Louis laughed.

"I mean, writing and storytelling," Sean mentioned.

"Well you can't be that good or you wouldn't be jobless," Louis joked.

"Man, that's messed up," Sean defended.

"I'm just playing," Louis replied.

"They say a joke is truth wrapped in a smile," Sean asserted.

"Na, there's plenty of talented people who just haven't gotten their break. Hard work and a pinch of luck is all you need sometimes," Louis stated.

Sean just looked on. He was impressed with how wise Louis was.

"So I'll rephrase the original question. What are you great at?" Louis asked.

"Uhh, great? I'll say I'm great with people. Most people show me love. Everybody except this one dude, but he's nobody. Communicating and making folks just happy in general," Sean bared.

"I agree. The way my sister speaks about you confirms that," Louis recognized.

"So that right there is why you become a police officer. To help people because you're great at it," Louis coached.

"Wow," Sean said.

Louis moved the first piece on the chessboard.

"Oh, na, I don't know how to play chess, bro. I know how to play checkers," Sean said.

"No, I'll show you. Checkers is cool, but this is grown-man business here," Louis claimed.

"And who is this dude you mention that's just hating on you?" Louis asked.

"He's no one, just my brother's friend," Sean alluded.

Louis's face turned up. He was very intrigued and concerned about the comment. The fact that Sean mentioned it, but glossed over the issue, grabbed Louis's attention.

"Have you talked to your brother about it?" Louis questioned.

"No," Sean answered.

"Why not?" Louis asked.

"I don't want to make it a big deal," Sean said as he watched Louis set up the chess board.

"Maybe you should mention it in a subtle way. Just say, 'hey this dude always has something to say about me,'" Louis explained. Maybe your brother doesn't even notice it and he'll just get the guy to fall back a little.

"Yeah, that's true," Sean replied as he yawned.

Louis felt like he gave the young man solid advice. However,

Sean just agreed, in order to move on from the subject. He knew that Louis had no idea what kind of person Roland was. Sean felt that there was no in between once Roland received news like that. He would either completely dismiss it as "Lefty just being Lefty" or he would snap and embarrass Lefty. Sean simply wanted his old classmate to get off his back all the time.

13

EVERYBODY VS. EVERYBODY

"Look, I'm not killing no kids or no old folks, alright?" Ivan said to Roland.

"Ay, man, who the fuck gone be old out there at 12:00 at night, man? Shit, nigga, I'll smoke anybody. I just don't give a fuck," Roland retorted.

"There she go right there!" Roland whispered.

Roland, Ivan and Ramadan sat inside a rented vehicle quickly re-discussing their plans. They were parked several houses down from the gang leader, Mo, awaiting revenge.

"So, you gonna hop out and walk past her. Once you get past her, turn around and let it go," Roland instructed.

Ramadan sat in the back seat quietly listening as he stared at Mo from a distance.

"Don't hesitate," Roland urged.

"That's the broad that shot me, right?" Ramadan asked.

"Yeah," Ivan replied as he tapped on the steering wheel.

"I won't. Watch this," Ramadan declared as he got out of the back seat.

Roland looked at Ivan and then Ramadan with a sinister smirk.

"Ight, I'll go handle my end of the deal. You know what to do, bro," Roland explained to Ivan.

"True, bro," Ivan replied.

"You alright?" Roland asked.

"Yeah …" Ivan began as his eyes wandered away from Roland.

"What's up? Make it quick," Roland urged as he closed the door.

"Man, I tried calling you the other day. You didn't pick up …," Ivan explained.

"And … you sound like one of my chicks," Roland voiced as his face wrinkled.

"The whole hood said police came and picked you up," Ivan announced.

Roland shook his head in disgust.

"Man, that shit wasn't about nothing," Roland mumbled.

"So how come you ain't say nothing!" Ivan yelled. "If that would have been me, you would be calling me a rat."

"So, what you getting at?" Roland questioned.

The two men stared at each other.

"Them fucking pigs don't have anything on me. Or you,"

Roland urged as he opened the car door.

Ivan just watched his best friend walk off to handle business. Thoughts of losing football to the streets and going to jail filled his head. Sweat dripped down his face despite the car being cool. The football star for the first time ever considered leaving Roland.

Roland and Ramadan went in separate directions. Mo stood outside her trap house with one of her guys smoking a vanilla-flavored Black & Mild. From the one guy's outfit, Ramadan could tell there was no way he was carrying a gun. His clothes were too tight. The question for Ramadan was Mo.

The teenager was about ten feet away from the two targets. His hands were sweaty as he held the heavy pistol inside his hoodie. He felt anxious. It wasn't from nerves but from the anticipation of seeking revenge. He moved closer. Now two feet away from Mo, he saw her looking in his direction, but there was no way she could make out his face in the dark. Ramadan had his hoodie on his head. He walked past the two gangsters and decided to turn back around. Him turning around caught Mo off guard, as she anticipated the random youngster to just walk past her.

As Ramadan turned around, Mo could make out his face from the glow from the streetlight pole, but it was too late. Ramadan pulled out the all-black pistol, holding it with a glove on. The pistol was about three feet away when he pulled the trigger. The first bullet hit her right in between the eyes, and the second one cracked her skull. Two loud bangs seemingly shook the block, causing alarms to ring from three parked cars.

Mo's henchman took off running as soon as Ramadan let off the first shot. As expected, he didn't have a piece on him. In fact, he screeched out like a little girl. He wouldn't get too far. As soon as the runner hit the corner, Roland stepped out of a dark alley with a sawed off shotgun. He shot the man close range, sending him flying five feet. The huge bullet ripped through his stomach and knocked his shirt halfway off his body. There was no need for a second shot.

Ivan pulled up to the corner for both Roland and Ramadan. The two jumped in, and they all sped off. The trio had accomplished their mission. The car ride was quiet until Roland turned around facing his protégé.

"Now focus on your music," Roland said as he looked Ramadan in his eyes.

*

Sean was back at home watching the news, waiting for Louis to come pick him up. The breaking news of a police officer shooting an unarmed man in the back and attempting to cover it up was on six different news stations. Sean was quickly moving along with the police officer process. He had taken the physical test during the past week and was starting to study for the written portion. Part of Sean was still second-guessing his decision to pursue this career. Thoughts of 'What would Roland and his friends think?' crossed his mind.

Sean's phone rang. It was Louis.

"Come outside," Louis stated.

"Ok," Sean replied.

Roland was sitting in the living room with his father watching TV. While their relationship definitely wasn't mended, they were at least speaking. Roland had watched his younger brother, Sean, take a phone call and head outside. He got up and peaked out the window and saw a really nice vehicle pull off with Sean inside.

"Hey, Ro," Aunt Michelle said as she walked into the living room.

"Hey," he replied.

"You and your guys should come down to city hall this afternoon. The mayor is having a block party. There will be food and music," she explained.

"What's it for?" he questioned.

"It's a celebration. The city's murder rate dropped thirty percent last year, the fewest murders since 2002," she rejoiced.

Roland just listened on skeptically.

"How'd that happen?" he asked.

"Hard work and new police strategies. The police director has been going hard on these drug dealers and gangsters around here," she urged with an optimistic facial expression.

"Yeah, explains all the cops at night and on the weekends," Roland inserted.

"Yup."

"Well we'll see how long that lasts," Roland rebutted.

They looked at each other. It was as if they were having a dispute without words. Two different schools of thought. One that believed in helping people through the system while the other had no faith in the administration at all.

"Welp. I offered," Aunt Michelle concluded.

Louis handed Sean more study guide papers as he sat inside the car, putting on his seat belt. Sean was struggling with the material. He was making the mistake of answering the questions from his current point of view instead of the mindset of a police officer.

"Yo, I took the practice test several times, and I can't pass this shit," Sean declared.

"Na, it's not that hard, man. You have to change your mindset and perspective," Louis offered.

"What you mean?" Sean asked.

"Ok, so ask me a question that you've been struggling with?" Louis asked.

"Uhhh … All of them, but for example, they gave me a scenario. And in the scenario I was asked about shooting someone who had like a knife or some type of weapon or was a threat, and I answered I would shoot them in the leg. I got that shit wrong!" Sean explained.

"Well, you should have got that shit wrong!" Louis confirmed.

"Why? Why should I shoot to kill this person if they don't have a gun or I'm not being like attacked with the knife?" Sean wondered.

"Bro, remember this and remember it well. We are trained to aim center mass," Louis said.

"Meaning we are trained and ordered to aim for the torso when shooting at a target. And you can't assume this guy only has a knife," Louis went on.

"Wow, so y'all are trained to shoot people where their organs and shit are?" Sean confronted him.

"Yeah. Go to a gun range. None of the targets have legs," Louis reproached. "It's not about where you shoot. It's about why you shoot! Have a good reason to use deadly force. You have to remember at the end of the day, I have to go back home to my family. Have to! This cop thing's not easy. Ask yourself are you ready for the hate you'll feel from other ethnic groups and your own group, having a much more negative view of the world, being paranoid, keeping dark secrets, being stressed, sleep deprived and, worst of all, feeling isolated. Once you've answered that, you let me know."

Sean just stared at Louis, taking in all he just said. "Man, I hear you, but I still live at home with my family, so yes, I am ready for that!" Sean replied.

Both men laughed.

Louis turned up the car radio. He was listening to the AM station. On the station, the shooting of Mo and her crew mate was briefly reported. Along with two other shootings in Seth Boyden and Pennington Court apartments.

"Yeah, Sean, the city is at war," Louis said with sorrow.

"Who is it?" Sean asked.

Sean knew a little about what was going on in the streets, being so close to it with Roland. He had no idea just how bad it was though.

"Shit, everybody. Bloods versus Crips, Bloods versus Bloods, Crips versus Crips, cops versus both, blacks versus blacks," Louis made known.

14

BLACK AND BLUE

It was June 2009. Roland was back on a robbing spree with Mo out of the way. He was doing most of his work alone. Ivan would go stretches where he was too busy with sports, and Roland tried to keep Ramadan away from most of the crime scenes to let him focus on his music. He completely left Caesar and Lefty behind. Ro began to get annoyed with Lefty, and he no longer wanted to associate himself with the small crimes and recklessness. The final straw for him was being put in a situation where he had to get rid of the twins. He deemed them bad for business. He'd never forget that Lefty had introduced him to the twins.

Lefty and Caesar were bitter about the fact that the other three were doing things without them. The two of them were bitter but not broken. They were making their own moves. Lefty and his lackey were doing petty crimes. They were robbing teens and women, conducting credit card scams and stealing out of malls.

Roland's crimes were a little more elaborate. Roland and his two henchmen were setting up people who had real money: businessmen, rappers and drug connections all while trying to dodge the police.

The same detectives he'd been approached by two months ago picked Roland up four times since then. Everything they tried to pin on him failed. He had an alibi for every crime they accused him of. If Roland was going to go down, it would be because of someone else's doing. Someone else would have to snitch, and few people would dare. Not one time did they have evidence regarding The Bulldogs committing a crime, but with each police station visit, Roland started to second-guess the life he was living.

Just last night Roland was told that the Feds did a sweep on two other gangs.

"They kicked in the door on Bergen and Mapes and up on Hawthorne Avenue," one of the barbers uttered.

Still Roland and The Bulldogs carried on. Roland second-guessed his moves, but he figured he was smarter than the other gang leaders and after a few more hits, he would stop and disappear.

The crew still hadn't got their hands on Jerry Campbell, the biggest drug distributor in the city. That is, until today. Ramadan had stolen a Chevy Suburban for the job. Ivan bought sirens to replicate a cop car. Roland, well, Roland had spent good money on a police officer uniform. The plan was in place. They just had to come across Jerry and Doc's Mustang.

It was a rainy Wednesday, and Roland had Jerry Campbell's schedule down to a tee, the same way he memorized the armored truck schedule when he was a young lad. On Mondays, Doc, the muscle of the two, drove the car alone. On Tuesdays, the car was never seen. On Wednesdays, the car would come through one of The Bulldogs' main pieces of turf, Bergen Street, between noon and two in the afternoon. That was after their morning run at the park. Roland couldn't get them at the park. In fact, every place they stopped they were always met with a crowd of men. The only place it was just them two was in the car.

Roland, Ivan and Ramadan were posted up on Bergen Street in the fake undercover police car. It was five minutes to two in the afternoon, and Roland began to get worried. He was starting to doubt his research and question why the hustlers were running late. Just when all hope was about to be lost, he heard the roar of the 5.0 Mustang. The Campbell brothers came cruising down the street as usual.

"Okay, it's go time," Roland bid.

Ramadan was to stay in the car, just as back up, in case the plan went south. He looked too young to pose as a cop and would give away the set up as soon as they saw him. Ivan also stayed in the car, just in case they recognized the football star's face. Roland was going to walk up to the car alone and rob them. He was sure he would score some real money, but just the thrill of robbing them was what he was subconsciously fulfilling.

Roland sounded the sirens, after following the Mustang for fifteen seconds. He got out of the SUV and walked toward the sports car with one hand on his pistol, just as the police do.

"License and registration," Roland said to the Campbell brothers.

"Why are you stopping us, officer!?" Doc demanded from the driver's seat.

"Don't ask me any questions!" Roland warned.

Jerry looked on with a puzzled look on his face. As the leader of the two, he figured he would need to make sure that Doc didn't do anything to keep the cop around too long.

Roland decided to take action immediately before they could recognize or memorize his face.

"Alright, so nice and slow, put all y'all shit in the bag. You know what time it is, niggas!" the stickup kid said as he pulled out a garbage bag.

"Wow," Jerry exclaimed, chuckling.

"Yeah, wow is right. Jewelry, cash, cards, phones, iPad and that pistol on the backseat too," Roland continued.

"Move slow, don't try nothing stupid, Jerry, or I'll send this nigga's brains to Top's Diner, fuck boy," he urged.

Roland had more than enough stuff and was ready to go before someone noticed it was not a routine stop. He easily had at least $20,000 worth of stuff.

"We gonna get that back," Doc proclaimed as Roland walked away.

Roland paused. Thinking about his response. He turned back around and headed toward the Campbells.

"What? I been doing this shit for years, and ain't nobody ever get they shit back!" Roland reproached them, leaving absolutely no doubt in anyone's mind that he meant to keep everything and make their lives a living hell if he ever saw them snooping around trying to find him or their stuff.

"Matter fact, get yo ass out the car!" Roland yelled as he cocked the Desert Eagle back.

Doc Campbell squeezed his 6'5" frame out of the two-seater. Roland proceeded to do something he'd never done before: embarrass his target.

"Now take yo clothes off, nigga!" Roland went on.

"What? Lil nigga, you gonna have to squeeze that shit if you think you gone embarrass me," Doc declared.

Roland looked around. It was too risky to shoot him right there, so he settled for a pistol whipping. Roland smashed the end of the pistol into Doc's nose, causing the huge man to stumble to his knees. He then looked over to Jerry. The two legends locked eyes. Jerry just shook his head up and down, as if to say, 'your point has been received.'

Roland quickly walked over to the Suburban and sped off. The only thing he regretted was bringing Ramadan along. He remembered telling him to focus on his music, yet he had him join this particular heist since they needed a third person, and there was no one he trusted more than Ramadan.

*

Who is it?" Jo Jo asked as she peaked through the peephole

"It's me," Officer Louis whispered.

Jo Jo had fully recovered from the incident. She was still completely oblivious to what happened the night she woke up in the back of Louis's car. However, she no longer was asking him about it, as she was preoccupied. She opened the door, and Louis stepped inside. The apartment was small but clean and smelled of newly burnt candles.

He wore his hat down low, hiding his face from the neighbors. Jo Jo's hair was still wet from the shower she had just taken.

"Are you hungry?" she asked as she tied her bathrobe.

"Uh, actually I am," he replied as he took his pistol off his hip and placed it on the table.

"Perfect, I made enough for two," Jo Jo said.

The two sat at the table together. At first it was awkward, but Louis began to relax. He knew what he was doing was wrong, but it was different, and he was enjoying it. She made steak, potatoes and broccoli with cheese, all stuff he had before, but it tasted different this time around. Louis was done eating within ten minutes.

"So that's it?" Jo Jo asked as she began washing dishes.

"Uh, yeah, I guess so," he replied.

"Usually it's dinner and a movie, you know, but I'll settle

for just dinner tonight," she responded.

"Okay," Louis replied. He grabbed his pistol and hat and proceeded to the door. "Actually, I got time for one movie," Louis stated.

Jo Jo smiled and turned the TV on. The two began watching a movie from 1996 starring Martin Lawrence. It was twenty minutes into the movie when Jo Jo put her hand on the rookie officer's lap.

"Can I?" Jo Jo asked.

"Uh, what?" Louis stuttered.

"Lay my head on your lap," Jo Jo replied.

"Oh, sure," he responded with hesitance.

She put her hair in a ponytail and laid her head across his lap. Twenty more minutes into the movie and Jo Jo was making moves. The twenty-four-year-old moved her hand up his thigh onto his crotch. She grabbed his penis through his pants and looked him directly in his eyes for confirmation.

Louis just licked his lips. He was nervous, excited, scared and turned on all at the same time. Jo Jo continued her pursuit. She pulled out his already erect penis. She couldn't hold back her smile. She gently put his entire shaft in her mouth. Again, she looked him in his eyes. This continued for several minutes before he stopped her.

"Hey, hey, stop," Louis uttered.

"Why, did I do something wrong?" Jo Jo asked.

"No, not you," Louis replied.

"So what is it?" she asked.

"I have to go," Louis said abruptly.

The officer got up and grabbed his hat again. He was in such a rush that he nearly forgot his pistol, so he turned back around for it.

"So that's it?" Jo Jo asked.

"I'm sorry," Louis apologized.

He closed the door behind himself before the conversation could continue. Louis drove home all alone, just him and his thoughts as he pulled at his pant leg nervously. It was one of the worst car rides of his life. The path home felt so dark in many ways. All he could think of was his wife, Heather, and his daughter, Lina.

15
JOINING FORCES

Roland, and his two partners, Ivan and Ramadan, were laying low. Roland had been staying home for the past week ever since the big stick up of the Campbell brothers. The three were in the backyard lifting weights.

"One more rep, lil bra," Roland urged Ramadan as he bench-pressed his last set.

"Damn! That shit heavy, man," Ramadan exclaimed, wiping the sweat off his head.

"Ight, Ivan, you up," Ramadan said as he slammed the weights down.

As they continued their intense workout, they heard footsteps coming up the driveway. All three of them pulled out their weapons, just in case it was a threat. It was Lefty and Caesar. Ramadan and Ivan put their pistols away. Roland did not. It had been months since Roland and Lefty saw each other.

Lefty and Caesar walked up, both clearly high. Lefty was always high, but this time around, his high seemed different. It was more intense, and it couldn't be from marijuana. Both of them were breathing hard, muscles twitching, pupils dilated with blistered lips. They were high off crack cocaine.

"What's good, bro?" Lefty asked sarcastically to Roland.

"What up?" Roland said as he shook his head in disgust.

"Word around town, y'all niggas eatin' good. I guess that explains all the guns being out," Lefty report sneeringly.

Ramadan and Ivan both just looked at Roland to see his reaction.

"What you talking about Lefty?" Roland asked.

"What I'm talking about …" Lefty repeated swiftly.

"Man, the Campbell brothers got robbed on Bergen Street and have been tearing up the city trying to figure out who did it. I recall us talking about getting them before," Lefty threatened.

"Bro, you are trippin," Ivan interrupted.

"Shut up, Ivan, you never been good at lying, nigga. Fake ass thug," Lefty berated him just as he'd always minimized everything that Ivan had to say even before bringing in the twins and split the gang up.

"Watch your mouth," Ivan said as he stepped closer to his former friend.

Testosterone and tension were at an all-time high.

"Man, get the fuck out of my yard," Roland declared.

Everyone stopped in their tracks. They all knew Roland was serious.

"Fuck, y'all niggas," Lefty said, backing up keeping the trio in his sight.

Lefty and Caesar headed out. Caesar stuck his middle finger up at the three, and Lefty did a shooting gun motion toward Ivan. As the two junkies walked down the driveway, Sean walked up it, and Lefty's shoulder collided smack into Sean, hitting him hard in his right shoulder. Sean just looked at Lefty confused. He was confused that his former classmate did not speak and instead had the nerve to bump him like that.

Sean looked back at Lefty. Lefty looked at Sean and again made a gun shooting hand motion toward him this time.

"Yo, what the fuck is up with Lefty?" Sean asked Roland.

"That's not Lefty anymore," Roland replied as he stared at his old pal departing.

"Anyway, I got something to tell you," Sean said as he pulled Roland off to the side.

"What's good, bro?" Roland asked.

"I got accepted into the police academy. I leave in about a week," Sean said stuttering.

Roland just gazed at Sean. His eyes began to water a little.

"Wow, that's what's up!" Roland said ecstatically.

Sean took a sigh of relief.

"A, yo, Sean got into the police academy," Roland yelled to Ivan and Ramadan.

"Word? Congrats!" Ivan and Ramadan replied.

All three gangsters were genuinely happy for Sean.

"My nigga, we poppin bottles tonight for you," Roland said.

"Before, we turn up, I have to tell Angel and her family. They helped me with this process," Sean declared.

"That's cool, bro. Tell Auntie and your pops too," Roland replied.

"Oh, he just my pops?" Sean laughed.

"Our father, whatever," Roland said.

They both laughed.

Sean texted both Angel and Louis. They were both at their parent's house. Sean headed over there to share the news with them.

He drove his aunt's car. The same car she would refuse to let Roland drive. When Sean arrived, Angel was already sitting outside listening to music.

"Hey!" Sean said as he got out of the car.

"Hi!" Angel replied.

The two embraced each other with a hug and a long kiss.

"You said you had something to tell me. So what is it?" Angel asked.

"So, I got accepted into the police academy," Sean said, grinning from ear to ear.

His teeth practically coming out of his face.

"That's awesome! I'm so proud of you. I knew you could do it," Angel yelled as she jumped up and down.

"Yeah, exactly that. You knew I could do it," Sean relished everything she did for him to get to this point. He couldn't believe that only a few months ago all he did was help her save a paper from a computer that wasn't plugged in, and through it all she had faith in him. She really believed in him, introduced her to Louis, and it had made all the difference in boosting him up to think he could do it.

"You believed in me. Gave me confidence when I had little, and I owe that to you," he confided, genuinely hoping that somehow someday he'd be able to return the precious moments she'd spent pushing him forward.

"Aw, baby, you are very smart and ambitious. Hard work and faith is all you need sometimes," Angel said.

They hugged and kissed again. The couple's passion matched one another's. Their happiness danced together.

"Hey, hey, hey, enough of all that kissing!" Louis bellowed as he walked out the front door.

"Tell him, baby, tell him," Angel urged.

"Tell me what?" Louis yelled.

"So I got into the police academy," Sean voiced with excitement.

"Wow, bro, that's good!" Louis replied, smiling.

Sean released his hold on Angel and walked to Louis. The two men hugged, both men squeezing the other tightly while rocking back and forth. Their hug brought Angel to tears.

"Thank you. You've also helped me get this far. While I know I'm only halfway there, I have to say, you have become a big brother to me and the person I look up to," Sean expressed.

Louis looked Sean in his eyes and shook the young man's hand firmly.

"You are such a responsible young man, and I'm also happy that my sister has chosen you as a partner," Louis replied.

"Alright, alright, enough of the small talk! La comida està hecha," Angel shouted.

"What does that mean?" Sean asked.

"Just come eat." Louis chuckled.

*

Meanwhile, Lefty was thinking of a plan. The plan would alter everyone's life. He headed to the park in hopes of seeing the Campbell brothers. Three hours went by as Lefty and Caesar waited for the purple Mustang to appear. His patience paid off. The 5.0 engine could be heard coming through the park.

Lefty quickly jumped off the crate he was sitting on and walked into the middle of the street. The car was about sixty feet away and did not appear to be slowing down one bit. Lefty was still a little high on crack and just stood in the road like a statue.

"Yooo, move, bro. He's not stopping," Caesar yelled from the sidewalk.

The car was twenty feet away when the driver finally began to slam on his brakes. Smoke and tire burns filled the park's road. The car stopped about two feet away from Lefty. Both front windows rolled down, and out came one gun in each hand. The guns were pointed towards Lefty.

"How you want to die today?" Jerry Campbell said from the passenger seat.

"No, it's not like that," Lefty said as he raised his hands.

"You got us fucked up if you think you about to get us," Doc Campbell yelled.

"Not like that at all," Lefty said.

"So what you selling candy, then, nigga?" Jerry asked.

"And who the fuck is that black ass boy there?" Doc demanded.

"That's my homie Caesar. He's good people," Lefty replied.

"So get to the point," Jerry said as he waved his pistol.

"What if I told you I knew who robbed y'all the other day?" Lefty declared.

"What if I said you was full of shit," Jerry said as he cocked the gun.

"Whoa, whoa, whoa!" Caesar yelled from the sidewalk.

"Come on, man, I did a lot of robbing in my day, but even I know better than to try y'all," Lefty replied.

The two men in the vehicle just looked at each other.

"Nobody in New Jersey or New York would try and steal from the Campbell brothers. Nobody except Roland Webb," Lefty explained.

The brothers put their pistols down. Down, but not away.

"Yo, search these young boys, Doc," Jerry ordered angrily. Jerry, despite being a drug kingpin, was calculated and tactical. He spoke with a slight raspy tone.

Doc got out of the vehicle and began to pat down Lefty and

Caesar. Neither one of them had weapons.

"Get in the car," Jerry directed.

Lefty and Caesar both looked over their shoulders and got into the Mustang.

"Let me see both of y'all driver's license," Jerry urged.

Both Lefty and Caesar were confused.

"Why?" Caesar asked.

"Don't ask no more question, youngin,'" Doc said as he placed his bear-like hand on Caesar's knee.

Lefty handed over his license. Caesar was still a minor and did not have one. Jerry took Lefty's identification and took a picture of it on his phone.

"So, I just sent this picture to one of my shooters. And I told him if anything goes wrong, he is to go to this address and hang one person living there every day until there's no one left. With that said, now we can do business," Jerry stated.

Everyone in the car was silent after that.

"So, who is this cock sucker, Roland Webb, and why are you snitching on him?" Jerry asked.

"He a stickup legend. I'm surprised y'all don't know him by now. He's like that. Not one of those social media thugs. He will rob or kill you."

"Sounds like a guy I should've hired," Jerry said smiling.

"Na, bra, this nigga ain't nothing to play with. He got all kinds of bodies, man. These kids I was cool with were talking too much and ain't nobody seen them in weeks. And I'm sure Roland did it," Caesar urged.

"Alright, so this nigga got y'all scared," Doc said.

There was a pause in the conversation.

"Man, this nigga just has to go," Lefty replied.

"So, kill him, then. What y'all need a strap?" Jerry asked.

"Y'all not listening, man," Lefty said.

"Alright so clearly you came to us because you want us to do him. Why you want him dead so bad? He rob you too, lil cuz?" Jerry questioned.

"Na, he ain't rob me," Lefty replied. "He just … not who I thought he was," Lefty said as he took his dreads out of a ponytail.

"Interesting. But to be honest with you, I could buy all that shit I lost again … ten times. Why risk the men and more importantly, why bring the attention that may come with going after him?" Jerry asked Lefty as he lit a cigar.

Lefty hesitated. As he predicted, Jerry wouldn't go after Roland just to get back some materialistic things he could easily buy. So he took a page out of Roland's book and had a plan B.

"If getting your stuff back is not enough, I've been sitting on a move for quite some time now," Lefty brought up.

Everyone in the car was quiet. Even Caesar seemed surprised, not sure what Lefty was going to say.

"Roland's been in the way of a bigger move I've been working on. Y'all know Harry and Kellie Sweeney?"

"Yeah, they're major players in the drug game," Jerry said as he looked over at his brother in slight confusion.

"Yeah. Major as in they make up the rest of New Jersey's

work, outside of your turf," Lefty said swiftly as he wiped sweat from his brow.

"So, what you getting at?" Jerry questioned.

"I've been in contact with them. Working on how we could come together and create a bigger coalition throughout the whole state. New Jersey is small, and we need to stick together instead of going at each other's throats. Join forces like some of them Italian mobs be doing and shit," Lefty proposed.

Jerry looked on puzzled. Lefty was smarter than he had assumed.

"Prove you be in contact with the Sweeneys," Jerry urged as he leaned in.

Lefty looked at both the Campbell brothers. He then looked at Caesar. This was the moment of truth, as he knew his next decision could very well mean life or death.

Lefty reached into his pocket. He pulled out his phone and began to dial.

"Hello?" a female voice answered.

"Hey, Kellie, did I leave my hat at the house?" Lefty asked.

"Let me check," the voice replied.

"Please do. Can you just call me back if you see it? Thank you," Lefty said as he hung up the phone.

Everyone in the vehicle was quiet once more.

"How do we know that was Kellie fucking Sweeney?" Doc interjected.

"I'm going to take a chance and assume you wouldn't be stupid enough to fake that call understanding what's at stake here," Jerry interrupted as he leaned in closer to Lefty.

"Of course not," Lefty urged.

"And I'm assuming Roland is in the way of a coalition being done, huh?" Jerry questioned as he fixed his tie.

"Yeah. All he wants to do is rob and kill. A person like him don't see the benefits in people uniting."

"Let's get him out the way and then we can talk business," Lefty offered.

Jerry and Lefty just locked eyes. There was some sort of understanding.

"You got a lot of anger in your heart. Why are you coming to me now though if he's been a monster for so long?" Jerry asked.

"There's no better time than the present," Lefty replied.

"Look, there's some ways we can help each other expand and distribute more."

"Yeah, I know, but Ro don't. His armed robbery rep's got him unable to get into any of the city's distributing network. … I know, because he's never going to ease up their worries that the city's patrolling and tech aren't going to find their way to their doorways with the way Ro go about things."

"But you're in?"

"I can hook you up."

"Say no more … So, where can I find him?" Jerry responded.

16
NO RETURN

It was the dead middle of summer. Ninety-three degrees was a nightmare for Newark residents. Kids played in the fire hydrant, and all the gangs in the city were outside stirring up trouble.

The start of the new school year was right around the corner. Ivan was just finishing up helping with the youth football team that his Coach Bowers had recommended during the season. Through Roland's advice, Ivan decided to take his assistant coach up on his offer to help coach younger players on the weekend. He decided to ignore the fact that Coach Bowers was secretively gay. He'd talked it out even with Roland who didn't really focus on the coach but more on his friend Ivan. Roland advised Ivan, telling him that people will always make jokes, but he should do whatever he thought he'd thank himself for doing ten years from now. That statement was enough for Ivan to give his coach and the idea a chance.

Ivan walked to his new rental car and opened the door. He began to take off his top layer, which was covered in sweat from the practice. Lefty came from behind a large oak tree near Ivan's car.

"What's good, superstar?" Lefty said.

"What the fuck you want?" Ivan replied.

Lefty walked closer. He wore a dirty black tank top, black jeans and matching sneakers. None of his clothing had logos or labels on them. A hat covered his short dreadlocks.

"You know the difference between you and I?" Lefty asked.

Ivan just stared at Lefty as he cracked his knuckles.

"Na, you don't," Lefty dubiously shared his doubts.

Ivan tightened his pants, waiting for his old pal to make a move.

"You know, on my way over here, I thought about what I was going to say to you before I killed you," Lefty stated coldly. "I was trying to come up with something cool to say, but honestly, it's not much to you. You just a typical dumb nigga that had a chance to make it but wanted to portray something he's not. Never portray something you're not."

"So, you came to fight?" Ivan asked as he took off his shirt.

"What? This ain't back in the day!" Lefty responded.

Lefty pulled out a silver .45 caliber handgun with a silencer. Ivan's eyes jolted open. He tried to jump in the car and speed off, but it was too late. Lefty shot him in his arm, chest and throat with three pulls of the trigger. He walked up to his former friend and shot him in the side of the head for good measure. Nothing was pumping through Ivan's heart anymore, and Lefty's cold heart seemed to be beating faster. Lefty had held up his end of the deal, eliminating Roland's ally and the only potential person who could retaliate. It was now Jerry's turn to make a move on Roland.

*

On the other side of town, Louis was headed over to Jo Jo's place again. The rookie officer quietly knocked on the door as usual.

"Who is it?" Jo Jo asked as she peaked through the peephole.

"Lou," he said softly.

She opened the door, and Louis stepped in. His hat was on backwards. Jo Jo had on silk pajamas.

"I assumed you was hungry, so I made extra," she offered as she combed her long hair.

"Na, I'm good," he replied as he took his pistol off his hip and placed it on the table. "Have a seat. We need to talk."

The two sat at the table together. There was an unusual tension between them.

"What could you want to talk about, Louis?" she asked nervously. "We haven't spoken in days since you came over here and got what you wanted." She insinuated more than she intended, and for a moment she recognized that she was just getting catty in case he was going to hurt her feelings.

"What? I never asked for that or any of this!" Louis disputed.

"I thought we had something special. From the time I met you, the hospital visits, hanging out together and intimate moments we shared. How you just ignore me for days after all of that?" Jo Jo accused him, wavering between distrust and her own feelings from being neglected by him so early in what she wanted to be a longer relationship.

"I had a lot on my mind," he answered.

"A lot, like what? That's what I'm here for. Honestly, Louis—" she fluctuated for a moment between her desire to tell him how crazy he'd made her about him and the little voice inside that kept telling her it was too soon to have such strong feelings in the first place. "I love you," she blurted out, and her feelings took over.

The two just looked at each other in silence. Three whole minutes went by, and the only thing you could hear was the leaking faucet from Jo Jo's old bathroom.

"We didn't meet the way you think we met, and I'm not who you think I am," Louis declared.

"What?" she asked, bracing herself because she hadn't even suspected that anything about him should have given her pause or reason to harbor any suspicions.

"We did not meet how you think we met, and I am not the person who you think I am!" he repeated loudly.

"Then, you care to clarify, please?"

He hesitated as he looked at her awaiting eyes, eyes he'd fallen for and that beautiful pouty mouth that made him crazy about her. He could see fear creep over her. "We met that night in the backseat of my vehicle because I hit you with my car going twenty miles per hour driving home drunk," Louis said as tears ran down his face falling to the floor. "And my name is Louis Little. I'm a married man with a four-year-old beautiful daughter that I have to go home to," he broke out the truth as he began to wipe his face.

The pressure had been killing him, and it was finally lifted, although he had no idea how he could have lost all of his scruples so easily, when all he had wanted to do was do what was right on the job. He felt disgusted with himself, and as he looked at Jo Jo, he remembered how badly he'd wanted to prove that he was as accountable as he could be in all aspects of his life. He'd been the one trying to fight for police accountability and now here he was?

Man, none of us are up enough on our luck, just spiraling, he thought to himself. *One thing leads to another, and the next thing you know you might lose everything because you're still reeling from other shit going on inside that you haven't dealt with. Just like I told that young man dating my sister, you always have to have a good reason to use deadly force, but where's the reason in this here? Fuck! I told Sean that it was a matter of getting back home to my family! I told that person holding the video camera to share that footage about an innocent man being shot in the back, and this is what I'm doing with all my talking about honesty and shit? How am I going to try to incriminate another and act so faultless?*

The weight of that memory fell on him hard as he faced Jo Jo, who just stared at him slowly. Time seemed to stand still. He could barely account for all of this to himself, and guilt began to rack him inside as he wondered at how he was ever going to get back on track. He hated seeing Jo Jo fill with pain, and he could barely manage the emotions stirring inside of himself.

Jo Jo sat at the table, overwhelmed with all she just heard.

"So that's it?" Jo Jo asked as she put her hair in a ponytail.

"Yeah, I'm sorry. That's it," he mumbled.

"That's it? Just like that you're done?" she asked again.

"I know it hurts," Louis replied.

"I said I love you, and you tell me you nearly killed me, and on top of that you are married with a child?" she reflected angrily.

Louis had nothing to say. They both were silent. The only noise in the home was the TV. The same movie was on from the last time he was over. It was *A Thin Line Between Love and Hate.* It was near the end of the movie, as actor Martin Lawrence was falling through a window into a pool as he tried fighting off his deranged lady friend.

"I have to go now. I have to go for good," Louis mumbled.

He turned his cap to the front and proceeded to the door. He was in such a rush that he started heading out without his weapon. He touched the side his gun usually rested on and noticed that it wasn't there. Before he could turn around, it was too late. A loud blast filled the room as one deadly bullet blasted through the back of his head and knocked his hat off to the floor. He collapsed against the front door that he'd almost reached.

Jo Jo had never shot a gun before, but she managed to kill Louis with one shot. She took the pistol, inserted the entire barrel into her mouth, and pulled the trigger. Her blood splattered all over the red and white Converse sneakers she'd worn the day she'd crossed the street and met the man she'd so quickly fallen in love with.

17
WAR IS BUSINESS

Black suit, black dress. Black suit, black dress. Black suit, black dress … that's what everyone wore to Officer Louis's funeral. On the other hand, everyone wore whatever they pleased to Ivan's funeral. Some wore tank tops to stay cool through the heat wave. Over three hundred people packed into the funeral home, for the rookie officer's burial. Just a quarter of that attended the football star's passing.

Roland walked away among the procession of people who weren't immediate family, leaving Ivan's sister, brother and parents sobbing at his friend's bare gravesite. Despite how the community had come together, Roland couldn't shake the feeling of wanting to do something for Ivan's family, but he knew he'd already done enough, and he had very little he could do besides maybe leave them alone in their despair.

Mr. Marshall was suddenly walking alongside of Roland.

"Not too many people care about another young negro getting buried," Mr. Marshall whispered as he placed his hand on Roland's shoulder. "I saw you at the cop's funeral this morning ... did you know him too?"

"I met him once. Crazy thing is, Sean knew him well. He's dating the cop's sister, and Louis helped him get into the police academy," Roland said.

"Yeah, I knew the family. I remember seeing Sean with the girl Angel at the ice cream parlor one day, and I couldn't recall how I knew her, but that was it," Mr. Marshall jested.

"That sucks. He got done by his mistress. His wife must have all kinds of emotions." Roland grew appalled at the way Sean's mentor ended up after all.

Mr. Marshall just shook his head in sorrow.

"And your friend. Sad stuff," Mr. Marshall grieved. He wanted to console Roland, but he knew it wouldn't be helpful if he came across as too heavy-handed.

Roland just stayed quiet. He was thinking of the right thing to say. "Yeah. Soldiers die in war, though. You got to be prepared for that," Roland figured.

"It's funny you mention that. I was listening to a talk radio show, and the topic was post-traumatic stress disorder. You know what that is?" Mr. Marshall asked.

"Yeah, PTSD. Ain't that what some people get when they come home from war?"

"You can say that. The problem with your statement is the

fact that it's assumed that it's only associated with war veterans, and that shouldn't be the case," Mr. Marshall inferred. "You know how many people in our urban neighborhoods have seen just as much if not more violence than war veterans? So how come the term PTSD isn't associated with those living in these violent communities? Just something to think about," the older man concluded.

Roland took in what he said, shook the hand of Poppa's old friend and headed out of the cemetery. *Another dead. What's everything I've seen?* he thought. Despite his statement being in the heat of the moment, he meant it. In fact, one of his many tattoos was the words "War Ready." Roland, Lefty and Ivan all shared that same tattoo, along with one that read "Death before Dishonor."

Roland reminisced about the time the three boys all went and got the tattoos. He thought about how much pain Ivan was in and how they teased him that he would get in trouble with his parents. A trouble and consequence that Roland and Lefty did not have to worry about. The gang leader's mind started to wander as he thought about how Ivan never should have been in a gang, and he did it trying to prove something to people. People like Roland. He also recognized that Ivan was pulling away from the street life. He wasn't as present as he used to be, and he was getting more involved with sports activities. It was too little too late apparently.

*

Meanwhile, Sean was at Angel's house trying to console her. He had attended both funerals and was exhausted. The late Louis Little's immediate family was all at the house including his wife and kid.

Every ten minutes you could hear someone crying loudly or arguing between family members. His wife, Heather, was torn. She was mourning the loss of her husband but simultaneously upset that he had an affair.

"Baby, I don't know the words to say to you because I would be broken losing my brother, but I do know that I will be here with you every step of the way," Sean said as he wiped away Angel's tears.

The two sat on the porch crying and exchanging stories of Louis all day long.

"Today we buried a great man. Not a perfect man but a great man," Sean told her as the sun set.

*

On the other side of town, Roland was walking home. Despite not shedding a tear, his mind was scrambled from the two funerals.

He walked past his old home that was now covered in char from the fire he set leaving the twins to die. A house full of memories, some good and some bad, but as of late, all he could recall is the bad. Roland realized that nearly every house on the entire street he once called home was either boarded up or aged. He shook his head and kept walking.

As he crossed the street, he spotted a young lady walking in high heels and business casual attire. He closed the water bottle he was drinking from and threw it in the trash can next to the recycling bin.

Roland jogged up to the woman and touched her arm, causing her to turn around.

It was Linda, his former classmate who was shot during their attempt to rob Mo.

"Yo, Linda, what's up!? I haven't seen you since you got shot!" Roland said with excitement and relief.

"Yeah, and I haven't been shot since I've seen you," Linda lashed back.

Roland's face wrinkled.

"I know you're not blaming me for that. Hell, who told you to go back there?" Roland whispered aggressively.

Linda stopped walking. She took a deep breath.

"I understand that ordeal was my fault. And I went back to the house, but damn, Roland. Can you take some accountability for what went down?" Linda said with passion and anger.

Roland stopped and paused. He looked at the ground and then looked back up at her. He noticed her scar on her neck from the gunshot wound.

"Well, I'm glad you're okay," he replied.

"Am I?" she said.

The young lady began walking once more.

"Yo, where you headed?" Roland shouted.

"To church!" Linda said without looking back at him.

Roland watched Linda walk away for a few seconds before heading home. He walked up the steps and put his key in the door, unlocking it. He pushed open the old rusted door and was struck in the head with the handle of a gun. Roland stumbled to his knees. He attempted to tackle his opponent but was struck again.

The attacker did not have a mask on, as he was not there to rob them. He was there to kill. The intruder was Doc Campbell. He wasn't alone. Two other men, wearing black clothing, held Roland's father and Aunt Michelle. Roland was caught off guard, and when the pistol whipping began, it continued relentlessly as it took its toll on Roland. He faded in and out of consciousness and hadn't realized what he had bargained for that day he'd tried to up his game and posed as a cop in a fake undercover police car. The last thing he heard before he blacked out was his aunt screaming, "I opened the backdoor for your friend with the dreads."

About ten minutes had passed by before Sean arrived home. He parked his aunt's car in the front as usual, put the club on the steering wheel as usual and pressed the alarm. He walked to the door not alert to anything going on inside. Sean went to put his key in the door, but the door was already open. He took two steps into the house. His father lay on the white sofa covered in blood. He had a gaping gash on his head and two gunshot wounds in his chest. He rushed over to his father, checking for a pulse and searching for any signs of life. Nothing. He was dead.

"Fuck! What the fuck!?" Sean screamed as he stood up straight.

He picked up a knife on the floor, a knife his father may have tried to use to fight off his attacker. Sean, confused and in shock, quickly walked through the rest of the house. Before he could get to Roland's room, he could see another body outside. On the ground in the backyard lay his aunt Michelle. She had a steady stream of blood coming from her head and neck area. Her shoulder appeared to be dislodged. Sean looked up above, and from his estimation his aunt was thrown off the roof.

Sean's aunt had blood underneath her fingernails and scratches on her wrist as evidence of a struggle. He thought to himself, his aunt had put up a fight. Fighting to defend her family to the end—a family that not always fully appreciated her.

Sean quickly wondered what her last moments were like. Her final thoughts. Never could she have imagined she would die in the same community she spent her entire adult life serving. Sean thought about the last meaningful conversation he had with his aunt and how that had to occur for a reason, as she was no longer here.

Sorrow, anger, guilt. Sorrow, anger, guilt … repeat. All those emotions ran through him as he left her side.

He slowly walked back inside the house after wiping away his tears. The floor creaked after his every step. He slowly turned the knob to Roland's bedroom afraid to see what was next to come. Roland lay there in his bed. His arms and legs were tied to each corner of the bed, as if he was crucified. Sean's older brother's shirt was soaked in blood. His hands and feet had six-inch knives inside of them. His stomach had two steak knives dug inside of him. Whoever did this did not just want to murder him, they wanted to torture him.

Sean's lips quivered. Tears ran down his face, falling to the floor.

"Na, na, na …," Sean said out loud.

"Not you, bro! Come on!" Sean said as he touched Roland's face.

Sean took out his phone and began to dial 9-1-1. Before he could press the call button, Roland spat out blood. Somehow, he was still alive.

The ambulance would be on its way soon, he reassured himself as he stared at his brother's tattoo. Death. Dishonor. War. Sean wasn't sure what was up anymore and how high of a body count there had to be to declare either a truce or some declared victory or unconditional surrender. He couldn't answer the questions streaming in his mind, and only could hope that Roland hadn't tipped anyone off about trying to go after Ivan's killer.

As the ambulance pulled away with his brother, Sean wondered how his aunt's murder was going to affect everyone who loved and adored her at the mayor's office. He'd only walked by even though she had asked him many times to come in and meet some good people and learn more about some of the new programs Newark was proud of putting together. Na, he'd just been caught up in trying to get out of this town, and now he could barely stop all the turmoil inside.

18
WHAT'S INSIDE YOU

Sean and Roland had been staying in a hotel outside of town for weeks now. Ro hadn't been seen since the summer by most. He was upgraded to stable condition and able to leave the hospital after being in critical condition for a week. His organs were intact as the two knives just missed his lungs. He had nerve damage in both hands and feet. The worst injury was to his abdominal area. Roland had to wear a colostomy bag after an infection formed in his abdominal. Despite the daily pain, he refused to take any painkillers.

No one knew where Roland and Sean were staying, except for Ramadan. Ramadan came by every day, spending most of his time nursing his idol back to perfect health. They had missed the news that the folks at the mayor's office had honored their father and their Aunt Michelle with a proper burial, although

Sean suspected someone had. None of them could risk going back to the house to find out.

Sean opened the door for the teenager.

"Ramie, what's good?" Sean said as they shook hands.

"What's up, big bro?" Ramadan replied.

"How Ro feeling today?"

"Slowly getting better. He did his first push up and jumping jack this morning, believe it or not," Sean declared.

The two both sat on the edge of Roland's bed.

"How you feeling, bro?" Ramadan asked.

"I've been worse," Roland said with a half-hearted smile.

"Any updates on Jerry? Doc? Or Lefty?" Roland questioned.

"Yeah, word on the street, the Campbells are shook. They can't believe that it was only two reported deaths from that day," Ramadan stated. "And as far as Lefty, na, no word. His little dick rider, Caesar, fled town once he heard that Lefty and the Campbells botched the set up," Ramadan explained.

Roland just nodded his head.

"Botched … them niggas fucked up," Roland judged. "After all I did for Lefty's ass. After all we been through. Fuck, nigga tried to have me killed. I got a fucking shit bag behind this nigga. Got my fucking aunt and father killed. He wouldn't have cared if you two was in there either!" Roland accused firmly.

The three just sat in silence. This was the most Roland said since the ambush.

"Just say the word, and I'll do 'em all," Ramadan said as he looked Roland in his eyes.

"If I let someone else do it, it won't mean nothing," Roland uttered as he pondered deeply.

The three men turned on the TV and began to watch an old gangster movie. Midway through the movie, Ramadan put headphones on.

"What you listening to?" Sean asked.

"Beats," Ramadan said.

"Beats? Oh you Dr. Dre now, nigga?" Roland joked.

"I told you, bra," Ramadan responded.

"So, you rap?" Sean asked.

"Yeah," Roland replied.

Sean looked at Roland, and the two brothers both burst out in laugher.

"Everybody want to be a fucking rapper," Sean yelled.

"All you have to do is get a face tattoo to cover up your gun wound, and you'll be in business, Ramie," Sean said as he pat the teenager on his back.

"Alright, y'all trying to clown me. You'll see." Ramadan chuckled.

"Na, I'm not doubting you. It's just we never heard you rap," Sean said.

"Some people didn't know Biggie was a rapper in high school either," Ramadan responded.

Sean and Roland looked at each other.

"Alright then, Biggie, rap!" Roland said.

"Now?" Ramadan asked.

"Yeah, every real rapper should always keep a verse on 'em,"

Roland said as he sat up on the bed.

"Man, I don't freestyle for free," Ramadan said.

The brothers laughed again.

"Okay … Sean, throw him that bag," Roland declared. "You told me you rap a while ago. I gave you some time to get your rhymes together. Now I want to hear something," Roland continued.

Sean grabbed a red designer bag and threw it to Ramadan. Ramadan opened the expensive bag. Inside it was a diamond choker chain and twelve hundred dollars.

"Go. If it's fire, you get it all. If it's ass, I'll just give you one of the two," Roland promised.

Sean stood up. Both Webb brothers practically salivating at the mouth, anticipating what they were about to witness. Either a laugh fest they'd never let down or true talent.

"I'm from where it's only two kids allowed in the store
The rest of y'all niggas could wait at the door
Some niggas get more opportunities than others
Some niggas come disguised as your brothers
I wish I was there when them niggas came knocking
A bitch shot me in the face and I'm still rocking
I'm still cocking
Blood everywhere, now what's poppin
But wait until they see Ro back from the dead
See a real nigga would've put two in your head
Knocking hats off like Lids
Bitch so nasty she tongue kissed my kids

Roland and Sean both looked stunned.

"Sean …," Roland mumbled.

"Yeah, bro?" Sean replied.

"Throw him that other bag on the floor too," Roland insisted.

The three laughed. Sean and Ramadan lifted Roland's spirits during his long road to recovery. He never felt depressed when they were around. When they weren't around, he would think about all his loved ones he lost and what he could have done. To snap himself out of those negative notions, he used anger. The idea of the pain he needed to bring his opponents quickly erased his latter thoughts. He remembered, he did not choose this life, he was just playing the cards he was dealt.

Each day Roland would give Ramadan a new challenge to help better him as an artist. He would have him rap on different beats and imitate different rapper's styles. Sean helped him revamp his social media accounts to help in his marketing. Roland paid for a photographer to come take pictures of Ramadan as well. Roland invested in Ramadan in a way he never had someone invest in him before.

"Yo, food run," Sean said as he stood up and stretched.

"Jerk chicken, I vote," Ramadan stated.

"That's cool," Roland mentioned.

Sean grabbed his late aunt's car keys and headed outside. He drove back to downtown Newark to a Caribbean food place. The aspiring police officer had his hat down low so no one recognized him. He understood the risk of being Roland's brother in current times. The food place had a drive-thru, so it was perfect. He pulled up to the old intercom and waited to be acknowledged.

"Hello," Sean said.

No response.

"Hello," he tried again.

"Come inside," the voice from the static-ridden intercom said.

Sean was annoyed.

"Don't shit ever work right in the hood?" he mumbled. He drove the car in reverse, parking it in between a van and a dirt bike. He walked inside of the food place. There was one couple in front of him. He was next to order.

"Let me get a, uh …,"

"You stood in this line all that time, and you still don't know what you want?" a recognizable voice uttered.

Sean turned around and behind him stood Lefty.

The couple quickly left out of the restaurant, having noticed Lefty as being the same person that terrorized them in another store in the past.

"It's sort of like your job hunt. You been alive for eighteen mother fucking years, and you still don't know what you want," Lefty said.

Sean just stared at his former classmate. He knew he was high off cocaine. He also swore that he had a lot to do with some of the recent murders.

"What's the point of killing someone if no one else knows about it?" Lefty asked.

"It's a shame what happened to Ivan and your family. With all that said, this is the part in the movie where you die. Don't worry. I'll send your brother as company as soon as possible," Lefty threatened as he took his hair out of his ponytail.

Sean could not hide his stunned face.

"Yeah, I saw that little nigga Ramadan lurking one night, so I followed him, and he took three sodas back to the hotel y'all hiding that pussy at," Lefty asserted.

"Now either he one thirsty little mother fucker or he ain't the only one up there," Lefty said as he smiled.

Lefty looked rougher than Sean last saw him. His skin looked darker. His hair looked unkempt. His clothes looked a little disheveled as well.

The store clerk hid behind the bulletproof glass. He prayed the surveillance camera inside the store captured everything.

Sean watched his former classmate turned cold-hearted psycho put gloves on and pull out his 9mm. He began to put a silencer on the weapon. Sean saw his only opportunity and threw a punch at Lefty, striking him in the face. Lefty took two steps back, dropping his silencer. Sean took off running outside as Lefty chased after his fallen suppressor.

The chase was on! Sean sprinted for his life. Lefty jumped on his dirt bike and took off after him. His messy hair blew in the wind. He maintained one hand on the handlebar and the other on his pistol. He was several yards behind the sprinting Sean, but he couldn't get a clear shot at him. Sean's hat blew off in the sky. He had never run as fast as he did prior to tonight.

His heart practically beat through his chest. He was afraid to even look back. He darted through the dark streets, dashing through alleyways and jumping over fences.

Every time he thought he was in the clear, he could hear the roar of the dirt bike closing in. Sean finally darted in another alley, but he made a mistake, thinking Lefty did not see which way he went. Lefty pulled down the same alleyway. He dropped the bike to the ground and cocked the gun back.

"See now, Sean, you know that saying … there's a light at the end of every tunnel," Lefty said as he turned on his phone light, exposing the hidden Sean. Lefty raised his arm and fired a shot striking the garbage can Sean was hiding behind. The missed shot made a loud bang.

"What was that?!" a neighbor yelled as they looked out their window from the nearby apartments.

Lefty looked up at the neighbor. Sean took that opportunity to take off running once more. Lefty chased after Sean again. He took five steps, paused and fired two shots. Bang! Bang! Both bullets struck the back of a parked vehicle, busting the window and causing the vehicle's alarm to go off. Lefty finally gave up as Sean got away.

As Sean sprinted away, he took out his phone and texted Roland and Ramadan, "Food spot isn't cooking anymore tonight."

Meanwhile, back at the restaurant, the clerk had finally come from out of hiding and went to lock the front door. Just as he was in the clear and had the door closed, a gloved hand reached through the entrance.

It was Lefty.

"I don't want any trouble," the clerk begged.

"Me neither," Lefty responded.

"But I do want the tape from your camera," Lefty demanded as his eyes scanned the store.

"I don't have access to it!" the man presented.

"Don't lie to me!" Lefty said.

He struck the clerk in the head with the end of the pistol, dropping him to the floor.

"Where is it?" he demanded.

Lefty cocked the weapon back, preparing to end the middle aged man's life in his own store.

He gently placed his finger on the trigger and took aim at his head.

"Okay!" The man surrendered.

The man came to his feet and walked Lefty to where the surveillance cameras were controlled. He gave over the technology for all recordings from today.

"Smart man. I wasn't here, now was I?" Lefty asked as he put away his gun.

"No," the sweaty clerk agreed.

Lefty took a piece of chicken and walked out of the store as if nothing had happened.

19

VICTOR FRANKENSTEIN

"Pass me those pills," Roland said to Ramadan.

"Na, bra, you been doing good without them this whole time," Ramadan replied.

"This shit hurt, man," Roland said as he touched his colostomy bag.

The two just stared at the bag.

"That shit is disgusting, my nigga. I'm sorry," Ramadan said laughing.

"Yeah, it is, but the doc's saying that it could be coming off sooner, rather than later," Roland said as he looked in the cracked mirror in the bathroom.

The legendary shooter was gaining strength every day and growing restless. He was itching to get back to the streets.

"Honestly, bro, this shit got me fucked up," Roland reeled.

"I'm gon' light these niggas' asses up, and then I'm getting the fuck from around here."

Ramadan just sat and listened. He followed Roland, but unlike Lefty, he had a mind of his own.

"Man, that's easier said than done," Ramadan stated.

"What's that supposed to mean?" Roland asked.

"Na, nothing. I just seen plenty of people try and get out or want to get out, but they couldn't," Ramadan explained.

When the idea of starting a new life away from war readiness ran through his mind, Roland realized he hadn't stopped to think about much lately at all. It was all he could do from letting his mind go in twenty directions. He'd been good at strategy when the three of the boys had been working together in their gang. They'd put it together themselves and developed a vicious reputation that kept everyone out of their way. They'd created a name for themselves and kept other gangs away from their turf. 2009 had become a bit tougher with all of the fed raids in the city on the 793 Bloods in the South Ward and 7 9 Tre, also in the South Ward. The increased tech and cop patrols in the streets from last year due to the mayor's office initiatives his aunt had worked on, pumping time and money at making it harder to get away with shit made him feel a bit scattered. And with the recent young guys who were cooperating with police and implicating some of the more notorious gang leaders in Essex County or trying to be social media stars, Roland was feeling some nasty heat now. Especially he felt an overwhelming dread because his aunt and his estranged father were dead as innocents that had nothing to do with anything with his gang. He felt a deep rage inside.

He'd seen what happened to Blue, but Blue wasn't as good as Roland was at all of it. He'd slipped up, and you can never slip up. These streets have an expiration date," Blue had once told him. "Your uncles used to be getting bread, but that all came to an end."

It hadn't occurred to him that Blue meant for him to heed any warning, because he wasn't thinking anything would ever bring him down. It couldn't.

Should I let it go and just be content with the fact that me and Sean were both alive? he thought.

Sean's protection mattered a great deal to him and had ever since they were boys trying to get by among people who were more interested in themselves than they were in either of them. Then his thoughts brought him back to the one adult who did try with him and Sean. He thought to himself, *How would Poppa handle it?* He figured his grandfather wouldn't want his family attackers to just get away with such a crime. He remembered what Poppa told him to do to Tony from his elementary class. That was confirmation to seek revenge.

His aunt had been working to help make Newark better and now Roland was the only one who knew how her life had ended. The police would have no clue unless Lefty snitched, of course. Maybe that would be a good thing to bring the Campbell brothers down? Na, the police wouldn't believe Lefty even if he did go to the police because he had nothing but street credibility. He'd killed Ivan, and Roland figured if the detectives were keeping their eye on him about the missing twins, someone might have noticed that he and Lefty and Ivan weren't a real gang anymore.

"Well, you ain't met a nigga like me," Roland declared.

"Yo, you know you never asked me how I felt about doing Mo. Being that that was my first. I for sure thought you would be wondering where my head was and shit," Ramadan realized.

"Na … I know how you felt. I remember how I felt after my first body. I know what revenge feel like," Roland alleged.

Ramadan just looked on.

"Man, the first person I did, was some nigga that went to my rival high school. He thought it would be funny to rob me with a bb gun," Roland attested as he stared out the window.

"Oh yeah?" Ramadan asked.

"Yeah, that clown had his whole hood laughing at me. Well, jokes on them. They still can't find that nigga," Roland announced, feeling justified.

Ramadan just took in the story. This was just another reminder of what his idol was made of. The two ended their conversation and began working out. It had been three weeks since Roland was attacked. His hands and feet still had scars, but they were about seventy-five percent back to normal.

Roland didn't have professional physical therapy. He and Ramadan were simply staying in the hotel hiding out, surfing the Internet for therapy techniques. Roland couldn't risk being seen leaving the hotel unless it was to go relocate. Their rehab sessions were intense. Roland pushed his body. Each day he would nearly pass out.

"Any word on Lefty or the Campbells?" Roland asked as he wiped sweat off his face.

"Yeah," Ramadan replied, grinning.

Roland's eyes lit up. "What?" he asked.

"So, word on the street is Doc's been running work through this warehouse all the way down in Camden. No eyes on Jerry or Lefty though," Ramadan stated.

"'Ight. I'll start with his big ass," Roland replied.

There was a knock on the door. It was Sean. He texted Ramadan and also did a special knock to let them know it was him at the door.

Ramadan opened the door and attempted to shake Sean's hand, but Sean was not paying him any attention. Sean was too busy looking over his shoulder making sure he wasn't being followed.

"What's good with you?" Ramadan asked.

"Nothing, just checking," Sean urged.

"Checking for who?" Ramadan questioned.

"Nobody specific, you know, the usual," Sean continued.

Sean looked through the peephole. His brow dripped with sweat.

"You've never come in here like that before. What's up?" Roland stated.

"Nothing. Just pack y'all shit, we need to go," Sean said frantically.

"Go? For what?" Roland replied.

"We been here too long. We just need to go!" Sean yelled.

Roland and Sean just stared at each other. The two wasn't good at hiding things from one another.

"Who knows we're here?" Roland asked as he lifted his mattress for his gun.

Sean just looked at the floor. "Lefty does," Sean replied.

"That's it?" Roland replied.

"As far as I know," Sean continued.

"Okay … let's go," Roland declared.

The three, all began to quickly put their belongings in bags. They were done in ten minutes like the time it had taken his aunt to drive to her work at the mayor's office. He knew that because he remembered the number of times she'd call before she left work asking him if he needed anything before she got home and often he'd ask for nothing. She'd already given enough.

"Ready?" Ramadan asked as he opened the door slowly.

"Yeah," Sean replied, back in the moment. He missed his aunt so much.

"Yo, how did you know Lefty knows our location?" Roland objected.

The room went silent. You could hear the inhaling and exhaling of the young men.

"What?" Sean asked.

"You heard me the first time. Close that door!" Roland charged.

Both Roland and Ramadan just stared at Sean. Neither could blink. They knew that Sean's next statement couldn't be positive.

"I saw Lefty last night," Sean mumbled.

"And?" Ramadan yelled.

"The nigga knows where we stay."

"So, he walked up to you and said, 'I know where you stay' like some 'I know what you did last summer' type shit?" Ramadan dramatized what he heard Sean telling him only to make clear that he wanted to hear the whole story fast.

"Na that's not Lefty's style. He always had a passion for flashing," Roland reminded everyone.

"When I went to get our food the other night, he came in there behind me. Pulled out a gun on me, and chased me for blocks on a bike. Nigga was shooting at me and all around me, man. I'm lucky to be here, man," Sean cried.

"Okay," Roland said as he hugged his brother.

"He admitted to setting you and Ivan up," Sean added.

"I know. Don't worry about him. Let's handle Doc first," Roland declared as the three walked out the hotel room.

The three got in a rental and sped off, going unnoticed by anyone. They were planning to drop off their stuff in the basement of Roland's and Sean's house and then get to work. Roland now had the goods on Lefty that the police might never be able to prove, and Ramadan wondered what was going through Sean's mind being he was going to become a cop and all. Ramadan was too afraid to ask Sean. He just figured it was better left unsaid. He looked at Roland and hoped they'd avoid getting any more attention from anyone. Anyone.

20

BOYZ N THE HOOD

"Yo, what time you think this fool Doc be at the warehouse? And do Jerry be there too?" Roland asked.

"Mostly late night I heard, like midnight. And Jerry comes through randomly. That nigga too smart to get his hands too dirty," Ramadan replied.

Roland and Ramadan passed a bottle of Remy Martin cognac back and forth on their ride to Camden.

"Yo, it feels like we been riding forever," Ramadan complained as he looked at his scar in the mirror.

It had been quite some time since he was shot in the face. Mo left a permanent mark on him. A mark that he wore proudly now, as it made him look more menacing.

"Damn, nigga, you never been off the block, huh? We still in

Jersey," Roland mocked him and laughed.

"Man, just pass me the AUX cord," Ramadan begged.

Ramadan put on some music. He began to blast some of Jay Z's old music, to get himself in the mood.

"That's my shit, but put this on," Roland suggested. Roland gave Ramadan 50 Cent's *Get Rich or Die Tryin* album to play. "That's that work. Now that shit makes me want to get the strap," Roland said laughing.

The two played gangster music sipping on cognac the whole ride to the warehouse.

"That's it right there," Ramadan whispered.

The two pulled over, dimming their lights. They sat outside for thirty minutes, waiting to see who all showed up. Three cars appeared with approximately six guys. One car was the GT Mustang belonging to the Campbells.

"Jackpot. Both of them niggas in there, cuzzo," Roland uttered.

"So how you want to do this?" Ramadan replied.

"Simple. We go in there blasting," Roland said as he cocked his gun.

Roland and Ramadan had a total of four guns. Two each. Both were wheeling a machine gun and a pistol. Both guys had one Draco semi-automatic pistol and a Glock with a thirty round magazine, prepared to shoot it out all night.

"Yo, I'll peak through that window and see what's in the nest," Roland whispered.

The two shooters got out of the car and crept towards

the warehouse. Roland jumped on top of a stack of shipping containers, while Ramadan kept being the look out. Roland saw it was a little more than six guys. He counted to ten, as the Campbells appeared to be meeting with someone. The four guys were Hispanic. Roland assumed it was their drug connects.

"'Ight, so they in there doing business with some papi niggas," Roland declared.

"'Ight, so they can get it too," Ramadan said.

"Na, we don't need another war right now. We let them leave, and then we go in there masked up spraying!" Roland stated.

"If somehow they survive, they'll think it was a set-up from their connect," Roland said.

"That's a great fucking plan, big bro," Ramadan said.

"But, why would they use black shooters if they Spanish?" Ramadan asked.

Roland paused. "'Ight, maybe you right. So smoke all them niggas, then," Roland said, chuckling.

Roland jumped down. He reached down and tied up his all-black Timberland boots.

"Mask on," Roland uttered.

Ramadan eased the warehouse door open, not making a sound. The two hitters went their separate directions. Both were wielding their Draco machine guns. They could hear the black and Hispanic groups discussing cocaine prices. The two squatted behind empty canisters, waiting for the meeting to end.

Five minutes went by. The meeting was over. The Hispanics

left, and the Campbells and their crew pulled out champagne and made a toast to "new business." Roland looked at Ramadan from across the room and gave him a nod. A nod that signified it was time. Time for revenge. The two killers jumped up simultaneously. Both immediately fired their semi-automatic weapons.

Sparks flew, as the bullets bounced off the metal-filled warehouse. The men went scattering. They were caught off guard, as only half of them had their firearms.

"Get down!" Jerry yelled as he ran behind his car.

"Pay back's a bitch." Roland bore down on the Campbells as he shot two of Jerry's men.

Ramadan took chase after one man. The man tried to get away but because his pants were around his thighs, he couldn't. Ramadan shot him nine times in the back. The shootout went on for two whole minutes. Easily over seventy-five shots were fired in the warehouse. Roland and Ramadan eventually shot and killed all four of the Campbells' men. The two shooters were down to their Glocks, as they ran out of bullets in the Dracos.

Jerry and Doc both shot their guns from behind their vehicle.

"You can leave, and we'll act like this never happened," Jerry yelled from behind the cover of the car. His brown Tom Ford suit was covered in debris from the warehouse now.

"Fuck you," Ramadan yelled back as he shot at the sports car.

Ramadan crept around a large pile of boxes to get a better

shot at the Campbells. From this point of view, they would take an unexpected shot from the side. However, Ramadan did not realize Doc had the drop on him. Doc was thinking ahead and saw Ramadan's play. He crept behind Ramadan in the darkness. He raised his weapon and took aim at the back of Ramadan's head. Before he could let off what for sure would be a kill shot, Roland fired two shots. Both shots, ripped through the back of Doc's huge leg, causing him to drop his gun.

"No!" Jerry yelled from a distance.

Jerry began to fire relentlessly. He easily let off twenty shots from his gold-colored pistol, trying to save his younger brother's life.

"Pay back's a bitch, Jerry," Roland said as he fired several shots at Jerry.

Jerry reluctantly jumped in his car. He knew the war was over, and he was on the losing end of this one. Jerry started the Hemi engine and left his brother to die.

"Bitch ass nigga, I would have never left you or Sean," Roland said as he took off his mask.

Doc's face turned pale once seeing Roland's face. He knew that today would be his last day on Earth.

"Help me get this big bitch up," Roland urged.

The two pulled Doc's large frame up and walked him to a chair.

"Sit yo ass down!" Roland yelled. Roland took the end of his gun and smacked Doc across the face with it. "Remember that, bitch!"

"Just kill me already, man," Doc said as blood gushed from his body.

"Just kill me already, shaking my fucking head," Ramadan ridiculed as he shot Doc in his other leg.

The man screamed in pain. He began to cry. "Lord Jesus, help me!" Doc screamed.

"I see gangsters get religious when they start bleeding," Roland whispered.

The warehouse door opened again.

"You killed two people that meant a lot to me," Roland continued. "But they meant even more to someone else."

From the darkness, Sean appeared. He was dressed in all black and did not have a mask on. Covering his face from a dead man did not matter to him. Sean stood in between Roland and Ramadan. They were three feet from the tied-up Doc. Roland passed his gun to Sean.

"Who the fuck is this? This nigga don't look like a killer!" Doc uttered as blood fell from his mouth.

"Take a deep breath, good grip and good aim," Roland said as he stood behind his younger brother.

Sean got into his stance. He put two hands on the gun and aimed. Sweat dripped down from his brow. His hands shook slightly. He made eye contact with Doc. He lowered the gun and took a very deep breath, as if it was the first bit of air he had in minutes.

"See this little nigga ain't no killer like y'all," Doc said as he began to fade out of consciousness.

"Let me do it," Ramadan said.

"Na, he got it," Roland asserted.

"This fool took away your aunt and your father, and you have the chance to make it right," Roland whispered in Sean's ear.

There was a pause of silence.

Sean refocused, bringing the pistol back up to eye level. He closed one eye and began to pull the trigger. Then he stopped. He couldn't. "This won't bring them back," Sean said as he lowered the gun again. Sean handed over the Glock to Roland and began to walk away. Ramadan put his pistol away.

"If you plan on being a cop, you better be ready to pull a trigger, nigga," Roland said as Sean walked away. Roland began to walk away as well.

"Today is your lucky day," Ramadan said to Doc.

"No, it's not," Roland denied. Without looking, Roland pointed his gun and shot Doc in the chest, killing him instantly.

"Damn, hit that nigga with a no-look pass," Ramadan corroborated, chuckling.

Ramadan wondered what was next for Sean. He wasn't upset at him for not taking the shot because he wasn't a killer. That lifestyle wasn't for him and that didn't make him any less of a man. In fact, Ramadan felt a little bad that Sean was put in that situation. A feeling that he assumed Roland shared as well. He wondered if he would see Sean much after today.

21
THE BLUEPRINT

"Crate and yak," Roland said as he opened the bottle of cognac.

"Na, I'm good," Ramadan replied as he wrote something on his hand.

"You sure?" Roland argued.

"Yeah, I'm trying to finish this," Ramadan indicated.

Ramadan was working on his rhymes. He was quickly progressing with his rap career. Coming out to the world about his music was refreshing. To hide a passion because of the fear of others' opinions was a tragedy to him.

Roland helped him with that as well. He put confidence in him where he had little. "What's the good of having a talent if you're too afraid to use it? Too afraid that someone will laugh at you or not like it. Fuck the opinion of others. Some will support it, some won't. That's life." That's what Roland told Ramadan, and he'd been writing more ever since.

"Yo, these dudes gonna come over here and want to hear you spit," Roland said to Ramadan as he noticed a small group of guys walking toward them.

"Oh yeah? Who are they?" Ramadan asked as he stopped writing on his hand.

"Some old heads from around the way. Two of them can actually rap though."

Five men walked over to Ramadan and Roland. They all shook hands, as the men came in peace. One of the men began to rap immediately after acknowledging them. He was a heavyset, brown-haired white man. His flow was hardcore rap. He had a slow delivery and a few jokes. The second man to start rapping was a fair-skinned, skinny black man. He had freckles and a low haircut. His rap style was fast and aggressive. He was very animated, which Ramadan liked.

"Let me hear something, youngin," the skinny man said.

It was now Ramadan's turn. The teenager paused for a few seconds and then delivered. He was prepared for his opportunity, something Roland always preached to him. He took both men's styles and incorporated them into his own freestyle, practically imitating/mocking them. The men were all impressed. No one was more impressed than Roland as he yelled and swung a towel after every punch line.

"Alright, alright, my client don't freestyle for free," Roland proclaimed as he interrupted the cypher.

Little did the rappers realize they had an audience. A crowd of twenty adults and kids had surrounded the lyricist. The last time Roland had this much attention from his neighbors, he was being hauled out in a police cruiser as they cheered. Roland took note of that as he smiled, looking around at some of the same faces that once were hoping he be incarcerated. The men all shook hands and exchanged contact information.

"'Ight, I'll catch y'all later," Roland said as he sat back down on the crate.

"You knew they were coming this way?" Ramadan pried.

"Of course. I told them to," Roland hailed. "Just a test. Always keep your tools sharp," Roland recommended as he touched Ramadan's head.

Ramadan walked inside the corner store for a snack, leaving Roland outside alone. He sat on his crate unbothered, with not a care in the world. He wasn't worried about the Campbells anymore. Doc was dead, and Jerry was shaken up and not even sure who did it. Mo was long dead now. And Lefty, well, Lefty certainly heard about Doc and wouldn't be around after attempting to kill Sean.

Roland kept his head on a swivel, but he wasn't nearly as concerned as he used to be. As Roland sat on his crate, his eyes locked on his phone, a figure appeared behind him. It was a man dressed in all black, from head to toe. He walked up slowly and put his hand on Roland's shoulder. Roland turned around quickly and reached for his hidden weapon underneath his crate. He stopped reaching as he recognized the familiar face.

It wasn't a threat. In fact, it was a pleasant surprise. It was Blue.

Blue was the first person Roland ever looked up to besides Poppa. He had not seen Blue since he himself was twelve years old on the day they had attempted to rob that armored truck.

"Bro, what's good?!" Roland said as the two men hugged.

"How are you my, brother?" Blue replied.

"Bro, I'm maintaining, eating good out here," Roland replied grinning ear to ear.

"I see," Blue said as he looked around.

"When did you come home?"

"I just came home last night. Just coming from the Office of Re-entry. They helped me with my resume," Blue said. "I said I had to come see my man Roland," Blue professed humbly.

The two men stood in silence just smiling and hugged again.

"I missed my nigga man," Roland evinced.

Blue's face cringed after hearing that statement.

"What's wrong?" Roland asked.

"Nothing. Just that word. It's just … unnecessary," Blue criticized.

"What word?"

"The n-word. See, my brother, you use it so much you don't even realize it."

"My bad. Well, if you need anything, let me know. I got money for you, and honestly I got something for us to do tonight if you need more cash."

"Oh no. I'm not robbing any more folks, Roland. That person isn't here anymore," Blue clarified. "In fact, Blue is an old … pet name. Malik is more appropriate for me."

"I never knew your name was Malik," Roland said.

"It wasn't," Malik validated.

At that moment Roland realized that being incarcerated had changed his former idol. He took a step back, and it became clear to him that Malik had fully converted to Islam from his mannerisms, clothing and name change.

"You know what, bro? More power to you."

"Brother, join me. Rather sooner than later."

"I hear you. But maybe you just going through an after-jail phase that I'm sure you'll snap out of."

"Religion and Islam isn't something you just snap out of or grow out of. In fact, it's something you grow into," Malik endorsed.

"See now I don't like to talk about what someone didn't do for me, but after those first couple months, you and everyone else I was running with stopped calling, writing and sending me stuff. Only ones that stuck by my side were my parents who I should have listened to and my Muslim brothers on the inside," Malik said firmly. "Now if this means this is where we part ways in life, then so be it. But remember this: Inshallah, I'll be here for you when you're ready, and at the end of the day, everyone wants to go to heaven," Malik said as he shook Roland's hand and kissed him on both sides of his face.

Roland just stood there quietly as he watched his friend walk away. His eyes filled with tears, but he did not cry.

"Oh, and, brother, I'm sorry for all the BS I showed you

or influenced onto you. You didn't deserve that," Malik yelled from afar as tears ran down his face.

"Yo, my nigga, who was that?" Ramadan asked as he walked out of the store.

Roland paused.

"Just somebody I thought I knew," Roland said. "Yo, stop saying that word so much," he scolded.

"What word?" Ramadan asked

"The n-word," Roland declared.

"What? Nigga, pleaseee!" Ramadan joked.

The two laughed and began to pretend to fight.

"Na, you're right," Ramadan said.

22

CUTTING OFF THE NOSE TO SPITE THE FACE

It was Christmas Eve as the year 2009 was coming to a close. It had been seven months since Lefty was last seen in Newark, until today. He was hiding in Georgia at Caesar's relative's house until they caught him stealing and kicked him out. Caesar stayed down south, and vowed to never get high again or come back to New Jersey after all the killings. Lefty had no place to go or hide anymore.

"So, who has the best dope in town now that Jerry took his ass to New York?" Roland asked.

"This white couple, believe it or not. They run it off one of those number streets," Ramadan replied. "If you trying to hit a lick, there's easier ones rather than run in a house with white people, shotguns and chickens and shit," Ramadan warned.

"One, no more licks for you. You a rapper. Not a stickup kid AND a rapper. Not like Ivan thought he was a football player AND a shooter," Roland lay down the law. "And two, if that's the best dope, and you said Lefty was spotted back in town, then he'll make his way over," Roland predicted.

A part of Ramadan lit up. Inside, he was happy that Roland continued to believe in him so much he wanted him to be done with the life of crime. "True. What if he sends someone else to get it?" Ramadan asked.

"Na, that would mean he would have to let them in on the cut. And a crackhead ain't sharing shit," Roland shared from his experience as he cleaned his pistol.

The two watched the house for days. They would mix up the times they went, sometimes in the morning, afternoon or night. There was still no sign of Lefty. It was the ninth day of watching the house.

"You sure this dude still gets high?" Ramadan texted Roland.

Roland sat outside of the trap house alone. He was fully healed and no longer attached to the "shit bag." He was physically prepared to deal with Lefty. Going through his phone looking at old videos, Roland came across videos of a lot of people who were now dead. He eventually closed his phone and his eyes. Thoughts of how he played a role in nearly all those deaths hit him. He sat in the quiet car, with his seat reclined and window slightly opened. It began to drizzle. Roland rolled his window up not because of the light rain but because the smell of weed started to drift inside the car.

Roland looked up and a figure walked by. From the back, the silhouette looked familiar, but it was hard to make out, as the person had a hood on their head. The figure entered the targeted house. Roland attempted to contact Ramadan, but there was no service. He waited for the person to come back outside. Ten minutes went by. Ten minutes that felt more like ten hours. Roland grew impatient as he tapped the end of his Desert Eagle against the steering wheel. He had been driving his late aunt's car since Sean left their house for the police academy.

The figure finally came out of the house. He lifted up the gate and looked over his shoulder. From the body structure, he could tell it was a male. Between the hood and rain, it was still hard to make out his face.

The person stood a few feet away from the car. Now was the time for Roland to decide whether to take action or not. He was still unsure if it was Lefty or not. Roland rolled the window down to get a better look. The man reached underneath his hood to make an adjustment. Dreads fell down on his face. It was Lefty.

"Ay fool, don't move," Roland said as he pointed his pistol from inside the car.

Lefty was stunned. For the first time, Roland saw something on Lefty he had never seen. Fear. Lefty looked bad. Clearly his locks had not been re-twisted in months. None of his clothing were name brand or even clean. He lacked any of his old jewelry as well. One would assume most of his things were sold to maintain his drug habit.

"What? You gone shoot me out here, in broad daylight?" Lefty asked his former friend.

Roland made a face of disbelief that Lefty asked such a question.

"Don't tempt me!" Roland asserted. "Get yo ass in the car."

Roland got out of the driver's seat and began to pat Lefty down. Lefty wasn't armed.

"Get yo ass in and drive," Roland said.

Lefty got in the driver side, while Roland sat in the passenger seat.

Roland pressed the gun to Lefty's small frame as he drove. "Try something and I'll send your mother one dread at a time," Roland stated.

Lefty just drove in silence.

"Nothing to say, huh?" Roland asked.

"What you thought I would let all that shit you did slide or I wouldn't find you?" Roland questioned as he smiled. "Boy, you a junkie. There was only one place for you to go. You ever watch Animal Planet, dummy?"

"My nigga, just kill me already," Lefty mumbled.

Roland struck Lefty in the head with the Desert Eagle.

"Don't use that word," Roland yelled. "It's like a cat trying to catch a mouse. The mouse can run in a hole, but even that won't save him. See, the cat will just wait patiently right outside the hole until that little funky ass rat comes out. And the rat always comes out. He has to," Roland said as he slapped Lefty again with the pistol.

"Hard to drive like this, man," Lefty said as blood ran down his face.

"Shut up, we almost there!" Roland said.

Roland was taking him to the park that was a ten-minute drive away, taking him to the same spot the police found Ivan's body.

"Pull over right there," Roland pointed.

Lefty reached for his crack pipe.

"Pass me those matches," Lefty said as he put the pipe in his mouth.

Roland looked down in the cup holder for matches. He lit the pipe for the addict. "Enjoy that," Roland said as he shook his head.

Lefty inhaled the smoke, turned to Roland and exhaled in his face. Roland squinted. And at that moment Lefty saw his chance. He drove the car into a tree. The crash was loud. The front windshield shattered, and airbags went off. Roland hit his head against the dashboard.

When he came to, he looked to his left, and the driver's seat was empty. Roland looked all around for Lefty before getting out of the car. He didn't know where Lefty or his gun were.

Roland crawled out of the totaled car. He stood up and looked around. "Come out, you mother fucking mouse!" Roland yelled.

Just when the cold weather wasn't enough, it started to rain harder. In fact, it began thundering and lightning.

"Let's fight. Man to man. Like the old days! No guns, no tricks, nothing!" Roland yelled as he scanned his surroundings.

Roland was confused at how Lefty could have vanished so fast after the crash. The only thing he noticed was Lefty's blood on the steering wheel and blood next to the driver door. There was no trail, as if Lefty never left. He began to think that maybe in fact he didn't leave. By the time Roland realized where Lefty was, it was too late. A gunshot went off. A bullet darting from underneath the car struck Roland in the foot.

"Ah shit!" Roland screamed out as he fell. Roland crawled and rolled in pain.

Lefty slithered from beneath the totaled vehicle like a snake. He spat out a tooth and adjusted his bloody dreadlocks.

"I never really liked this gun. Too big," Lefty complained. Lefty took the pistol and struck Roland in the back of the head.

"How does that feel?" The question seeped out of Lefty's mouth like a venom that struck Roland in his brain. "You are going to die exactly where Ivan died," Lefty said as he stood over Roland. "I thought I would kill Sean and then you. Not the other way around," Lefty said as he shot Roland in the shoulder.

Roland hollered in pain as his head throbbed. His all-black Timberland boots had a splash of blood on them. He lay his head in the dirt. Lefty reached into his back pocket and pulled out a lighter after he reached in his pocket and pulled out his pipe. He lit the crack pipe and began to smoke once more.

"And to think I viewed you as a big brother," Lefty said as he took aim at Roland's head.

Just as Lefty went to fire the kill shot, Roland threw dirt into his face. The shot still went off. For Roland's sake, it missed. Roland came to his feet and went after Lefty. Lefty tried to quickly wipe the dirt and blood mix out of his eyes. He squinted out of one eye and squeezed the trigger again. Roland was able to get his hand around Lefty's wrist, causing the shot to go sailing elsewhere.

Roland kneed his old pal in the groin, causing him to drop the weapon. Both men traded blows to the face and body. The fight became dirtier and dirtier, as the men used every trick in the book. They tried to gouge each other's eyes out, kicked and punched with low blows, and headbutted each other, hoping to cause severe damage or preferably death. The men brawled for three minutes. Given Roland's injuries, Lefty was able to keep up with him.

Once Roland managed to grab Lefty by the hair, in one sweeping motion he used all of his strength to slam Lefty on top of the wrecked car.

"Fuck!" Lefty yelped.

Roland wrapped his muscular arm around Lefty's neck and clamped down as hard as he could. He held the headlock tightly—so tight, he began to put Lefty asleep.

"Na, you need to be awake for this," Roland said to a dazed Lefty.

Roland limped over two feet and picked up the Desert

Eagle. He wiped blood off of the firearm and limped back to Lefty's motionless body.

"For the record, I only have one brother," Roland informed as he raised his weapon.

"I'm sorry," Lefty muttered with a mouth full of blood.

"Yeah me too!" Roland assured him. And with that, Roland fired a shot into Lefty's head.

Did the air that once penetrated Lefty's lungs abandon Roland also as he fell back out of breath, gasping, desperately clinging to his bloody leg, unwilling to face the possibility that the gunshot was heard and someone may have informed the police? He felt little guidance coming from anywhere. His singular purpose for their gang had left him as unprotected from the world as he'd been as a child. He looked at Lefty and wondered how could this poser, this fucking psycho, have ever gotten so close to him and his family to take away the little protection his brother, Sean, had depended on?

The wars he'd started, and now the stillness of the night seemed only to verify that the security he'd hoped to have felt from the gang they once attended to had left him as the only one, alone. Unlike the feeling of vulnerability that he once felt when facing the world on his own, this time the feeling was of complete and utter pain in the burning pit where his breath, this air he shared moments ago with Lefty, tried to fit in, but his lungs seemed to be collapsing in his body. It felt as though all the death, all the betrayals, everything he'd hoped would build his reputation evaporated and had entered the same place where Lefty's bullet had entered. It inflamed him, but he didn't feel like it charged him up, in fact it felt more like it had turned his heart cold. Cold as Lefty's. A siren passed by, and he ran for his car limping and bleeding.

23
VICTORY LAP

"Shit!" Roland said, gasping for air as he sat up in bed.

Roland was waking up in a cold sweat every day since killing his old friend, Lefty, five months earlier. The killer either had repeat nightmares of shooting Lefty's bloody face or dreams of them hanging out like old times. He never experienced this before, despite being responsible for numerous murders in his lifetime. He got out of bed and turned on his speakers. Some of the songs made him reflect on the times him and Lefty spent together. The times he, Lefty and Ivan all spent as a trio. He began to work out more to take his mind off losing his two friends. He added ten pounds of muscle from the excessive workouts. He also decided to shave his head, as his hair had been falling out from stress.

The last words Lefty had said kept replaying in his head,

"I'm sorry." Roland even thought about the fact that Blue, his older brother figure, tried to save his life, while on the other hand, he took the life of Lefty.

What kind of big brother am I, then? he wondered.

To cope with his depression, he thought about the fact that Lefty murdered Ivan and tried to eliminate him and Sean. He felt like his actions were necessary. He reminded himself that he had preferred going to Lefty's funeral, rather than Sean's.

Roland went through his phone. He looked at a picture of him and Ramadan. He felt a positive uplifting feeling, remembering the fact that he'd steered Ramadan in the right direction from a life of crime to pursuing a career in music. To overcome his internal battle, he reminded himself that it was just that: a battle. For every thought of how he helped Sean and Ramadan, there were thoughts of how he didn't protect his aunt and father. Those losses were hard for him to swallow. The ones that he viewed as innocent kept him up at night. They lingered in his mind during the day. Some losses or actions he could live with. He felt like it was necessary or he'd have become a casualty in war. He truly felt that Ivan, the twins, his opponents and even Officer Louis all played the game and unfortunately they lost.

The only loss that wasn't black and white to him was the death of Lefty. While Lefty became his biggest rival and got everything that was coming to him, Lefty was the monster that Roland created.

"I should have just steered him to a different direction," Roland mumbled out loud. "Man, he did some bullshit. Those damn drugs," he continued breaking it down for himself.

He wrestled with those internal disputes every day since pulling the trigger on his old protégé.

For the first time since Poppa's death, Roland closed his eyes and said a prayer. He simply prayed for peace, forgiveness, patience and mercy. He opened his eyes and grabbed his phone.

He saw a text. "Meet me at the spot" It was from Sean.

An hour later, Sean got out of the passenger side of a police cruiser. He walked over, and he and Roland embraced each other with a big hug.

"Damn, bro, we almost got the same haircut," Sean said as he took off his cap exposing his tight fade haircut.

The two men laughed.

"You look good in your uniform," Roland noticed.

"Thank you," Sean replied.

"Have a seat," Roland said.

"Na, I can't stay long. My partner is waiting on me," Sean stated as he looked over his shoulder.

The two men had small talk for several minutes. Roland asked him about the police academy and congratulated his younger brother.

"I hope they teaching y'all how to shoot people in the leg for once or at least tell the difference between a situation and a *life-threatening* situation, bro," Roland stated.

"Uhhh … we're going through some trainings," Sean reassured him.

The two just smiled at each other. Sean noticed the bags

under Roland's eyes. He asked his older brother how he was doing personally. He didn't ask about specifics, as he didn't want to know of any crimes his brother might have committed.

"Well, I'm not gone hold you up. But you know something, Sean? You are the only thing I've ever been proud of," Roland declared. "You're the only thing I brag about to others. I look up to you," Roland confessed as he wiped a tear away from his face.

This was the first time Sean had ever seen Roland actually cry. Sean began to tear up. "Ro, you will always be my big brother. I love you," Sean reciprocated in his reverence of his older brother, loving him unconditionally.

"I love you too," Roland replied.

The men hugged.

"Alright, you get out of here, man. Go save some lives or some shit," Roland said as he wiped his face again. Sean put his cap back on and headed back toward the car. He opened the passenger door.

"Okay, Officer O'Sullivan. I'm ready," Sean asserted as he put his seatbelt on.

"Took long enough, rookie," Wayne needled.

Wayne was quite devastated after the death of Louis Little and the fashion in which it occurred. He might not even have admitted it, but he learned a lot from Louis. He learned a lot about life. He was so moved by the loss of Louis, he did one thing he thought Louis would want him to do. Between the leaked video, him coming forward, and coming up with enough proof, Wayne saw to it that he had done the right thing, leading to the police officers being convicted for the murder of the innocent man at the park. Wayne felt like having a new minority rookie partner was a do-over of sorts. This was a second chance in his eyes to be a better partner and person to Sean. About a week into the job, Wayne had informed Sean about his old partner. To both of their surprise, they both had known Louis. That common ground kick-started their relationship off to a great beginning.

Sean reached into his pocket and pulled out his phone. He called Angel.

"Hey, bae," Sean said smiling.

"Hi," Angel said.

Angel seemed to be in good spirits as her smile was so radiant it could be felt through the phone.

"What are you doing?" Sean asked.

"Nothing, just looking at my resume," she replied.

"Oh really? That's good. You're going to start applying?"

"Yeah … I thought about what you said before."

"What I say? You know I talk a lot," Sean joked.

"You know, about settling for a job that doesn't make you happy."

"Yeah, if this year taught me anything else, it taught me that life's too short to be anything but happy," Sean articulated.

"I hear you, love," Angel said.

"Yeah, I find it crazy that you have the ability to push others to do more, but you somewhat settle for the position you're in," Sean explained.

"I know. I just don't know what I want to even do," she admitted.

"Well, like a great man once asked me … what are you great at?" Sean asked

"Who asked you that?"

"Your brother," Sean uttered.

The two both smiled. Angel chuckled and wiped away a tear. "Of course, he did. He always knew what to say," she praised her deceased brother. She always remembered how much he cared about using the right tone with kids and maintaining a healthy attitude about the difficulties that come with life and making a stand for oneself no matter how many people try to get in your way.

"Well, I'm great at helping people," Angel hedged.

"That you are," Sean affirmed.

"You know what, one of my aunt's old coworkers have been calling the house checking on me. I'm going to forward her your email address and see if there's any openings she thinks would fit you well at the mayor's office she now works at," Sean decided.

"Okay, I guess that wouldn't hurt."

"What's the worse they'll say, no?"

With that said, the two wrapped up their conversation. Angel had taken a few days off from work, making time to visit Heather and her niece. Losing her "perfect" brother in such an imperfect way had just been mind-blowing. And the fact that people knew the murderer was his mistress made matters worse. She thought she didn't care about what people thought, but she did. Every time she left her house she felt like people were staring at her. She felt like people were talking about her. Was she paranoid or precise?

Angel received counseling for weeks after Louis' funeral. That helped a lot, but even more so, the love she received from Sean was just as therapeutic. Not a day went by that the two lovers did not speak to one another. In fact, they began to rotate sleeping over at one another's houses. Neither got a good night's sleep without the other.

Just as Sean pulled away, Mr. Marshall walked out of the corner store. "Roland, my man," Mr. Marshall said.

"Hey, Mr. Marshall. How's everything?" Roland said.

"I won't complain. How are you?" Mr. Marshall asked.

"I'm good," Roland said as usual.

"Okay," Mr. Marshall said as he began to walk away.

"No … I'm not," Roland continued.

Mr. Marshall turned around. He had never heard Roland say anything but 'everything is great' before.

"I'm not good. Not good at all," Roland said as he looked down. "Pardon my language, but today fucked me up. What am I doing with my life, man? My brother started his career, another kid I know starting a career, everybody else is dead, or in jail, or heading there, or coming from there. And then, there's me," Roland acknowledged.

Mr. Marshall took a seat on a crate. He wanted to listen. He wanted so bad to pull whatever wreck Roland had been handling out of the young man's body, spread it out and take all the broken pieces to help him feel like he could be part of the community he was used to bruising and kicking just like he kept doing to himself. He hadn't had a nice word to say about Newark in all the time he'd known him, and he hadn't had a nice thing to add to making this city a proud place to be. He was making so many bad choices, and he couldn't get anything from life from the places out of his reach beyond the life he lived where sorrow and gloom had rooted themselves so deeply. His aunt, Mr. Marshall and others had tried to get through to him, yet he just couldn't see a way to do it. At times this attempted to break Mr. Marshall's heart.

"Me. My situation is even worse. I'm just stuck. Trapped! Just waiting here … to die or go to jail. I'm not getting a job. I don't even want one, even if I could get hired," he considered. "What I look like taking orders from someone for less money I'm getting now? Having some motherfucker tell me when to take a lunch break and shit. That's laughable. I'm just going through my days waiting for a joker to shoot me in the back or for the feds to come get me for good. I'm not dead or in jail. I'm just stuck waiting for either of the two. Let's see which one gets here first," Roland finished as he opened up a new bottle of cognac.

Mr. Marshall bit his lip as a tear rolled down his cheek onto the concrete.

"Son, I don't think you realize, it's never too late to do the right thing. Do what's right from this day forward. One day at a time," Mr. Marshall advised wholeheartedly as he put his arm around Roland. "In many ways, I failed you … Hell, we all failed you, this whole community," the old man said angrily. "It takes a village to raise a child, but instead this village turned its back on its son once he started to make mistakes. Damn it! Everyone make mistakes. If you live long enough you're bound to fuck up!" Mr. Marshall stressed.

Roland had never heard Mr. Marshall talk like that before.

"When your grandfather died, I was one of his closest friends. And I should have taken you in, but I didn't. That man did a lot for me, and I neglected to return the favor, and for that I am forever sorry, Roland," the older man declared.

A few tears rolled down both men's cheeks simultaneously.

"I know what he meant to you. What did he teach you, Roland?" Mr. Marshall asked.

"Everything," Roland replied.

"Yeah. Name one thing. One that you value the most."

Roland paused to think. "To protect myself but especially, to protect Sean," Roland responded.

"That's a good one. Probably the biggest one. And do you think you've done that?"

Roland stopped to think again. "Yeah … we both alive. He a cop …" Roland acknowledged with the first hint of pride Mr. Marshall had ever seen in Roland.

"I think that you believe that you've protected yourself and your brother because you've used force and violence to get your way out of threatening situations," Mr. Marshall said. "But real protection would have started before that. Real protection would have been preventing those situations from occurring in the first place. With the amount of money you came across, hell, you could have moved your family out of these slums. You could have set up a better life for your brother and daughter," the older man pledged. "So I say, maybe you misunderstood your grandfather's message," Mr. Marshall concluded.

The two just looked at one another. No further words were said. Mr. Marshall gathered his groceries and began to head home.

"Hey, here," Roland said as he reached in his pocket. Roland pulled out a pair of brass knuckles—the same brass knuckles he'd stolen from Mr. Marshall's store as a youth. The weapon, was the first thing he had ever stole, which led to his first act of violence.

"I've been waiting for you to return these for quite some time now," Mr. Marshall replied as he took the brass knuckles.

Roland stared in utter surprise.

"How'd you know?" Roland asked.

"What shop don't have cameras in this city? Plus, you wasn't quite yourself that day. Get back to being yourself, son," Mr. Marshall wished, deeply enough to look Roland into his eyes longer than he cared to, longer than Roland ever let anyone get face to face with him. "Never too late to start doing the right thing. And, of course, pray on it," Mr. Marshall said walking away.

Roland could overhear two men talking about a shootout that occurred between rival gangs earlier that day. The man said the two crews had been taking turns shooting at one another all summer. Roland just shook his head, as he was tired of hearing stories like that.

Roland watched Mr. Marshall slowly walk all the way home. He just thought about what he said. He thought about how Mr. Marshall walked up and down the streets of some of the worst parts of town without any enemies. And he thought about how sweet life must be to have that peace of mind. He noticed Mr. Marshall still wore the same red flannel jacket and khaki pants from years ago. That was what consistency looked like. And the fact that he could care less about what people thought of him wearing practically the same outfit everyday also illustrated a level of security that Roland could only dream of.

Roland sat back down and looked at the cognac bottle. The bottle was full, as he hadn't started drinking. He twisted open the top and poured the alcohol onto the pavement. Images of all the dead people he'd come across in his lifetime crossed his mind. He threw the glass bottle into the recycling bin. Just as he went to sit back down, his phone buzzed.

Roland had two text messages from two unsaved numbers in his phone. Neither message was from anyone he spoke to often. The first text read, "Yo, I got your number from a friend, heard you might be down to make some money." The second text, from a different number read, "As-Salaam-Alaikum, it's

Malik. I wanted to talk further with you about Islam tonight if you're free."

Roland paused after reading both messages. He clicked on one of the texts and began to reply back, leaving the other unanswered.

"Walaikum assalam. I hope I spelled that right," he texted back. Roland walked a couple blocks before turning on a familiar street. The street he was born on. However, the once familiar avenue looked quite unfamiliar.

There were a handful of houses being renovated.

He walked up to the top of the hill where his old home was. To his surprise, the charred unit was being looked over by two potential investors.

Two middle-aged men talked about the potential of the house out loud. They were unaware that they had an audience.

"It's older, but I'm glad we caught it when we did. It's still not too late to save it," one investor announced.

"We may have to gut the entire house and start over," the second investor said as he pushed debris out of his way.

"That's an option. It has some structural and support issues, but it's still a good house inside," Roland interrupted with a cracking voice.

The two men were startled. They looked at one another and then at Roland.

"Yeah? What? You knew who lived here?" the other man probed.

"... Uhh … yeah … you could say that," Roland answered.

Roland continued to walk up the road looking from left to right in awe at the changes being made to the street where he had been raised.

You winning, Ro, he told himself. *You winning. It's still a good house inside. He felt a little warmth stir inside him. You winning.*

—

ABOUT THE AUTHOR

Haneef Arbubakrr is a writer and author of the new novel *It Starts At Home.*

With degrees in both communications and public relations, Haneef already has an established career in sports writing. Now, after more than a decade in that field, he has pivoted to fictional storytelling.

It Starts At Home is Haneef's first fiction book and highlights his interest in intimate coming-of-age tales and modern urban stories.

Haneef lives in New Jersey with his wife and family.

To discover more about Haneef and his writing, please visit:

www.neefwrites.com

Made in the USA
Middletown, DE
10 July 2020

12518480R00154